# Billy the Elephant & Other Stories

OJ Francis

Published by New Generation Publishing in 2024

Copyright © OJ Francis 2024

First Edition

The author asserts the moral right under the Copyright, Designs and Patents Act 1988 to be identified as the author of this work.

All Rights reserved. No part of this publication may be reproduced, stored in a retrieval system or transmitted, in any form or by any means without the prior consent of the author, nor be otherwise circulated in any form of binding or cover other than that in which it is published and without a similar condition being imposed on the subsequent purchaser.

ISBN:

Paperback: 978-1-80369-579-2
Ebook: 978-1-80369-580-8

**www.newgeneration-publishing.com**
New Generation Publishing

# Billy the Elephant

# Chapter 1

The purpose of the meeting was allegedly to discuss their survival. At Kobe's request, all elephants young and old, and even the most ailing gathered under the ancient baobab tree in the heart of the tropical Ituri Forest. In the cool of the moonlit night, every elephant took its place some quietly but others glad for an opportunity to share. Kobe the self-appointed organiser of the meeting mounted the pile of logs that had been carefully arranged into a platform.

Kobe, often referred to as 'Wise Elder' was the oldest elephant alive in the whole of Ituri Forest. Nobody knew how old he was. As a matter of fact he himself had no idea as to what his exact age was. When asked about it, he would simply say, "I am very old. I was born long ago on a rainy night. That time my mother was visiting her mother." That left many confused especially as rainy nights were a common phenomenon in Ituri. Nevertheless he was really very old, so much such that his running was not distinguishable from walking.

At his age, Kobe depended largely on a team of middle-aged bull elephants, both for safety and survival. That was the purpose for which he had raised them. They roared and squealed fiercely by his side and tore to pieces anyone who tried to force their way to Kobe without permission. Not one elephant except Kobe had a satisfactory explanation to their violent character and dedication to him. But amongst the many rumours that went round, one was that he had raised them in seclusion after first castrating them. Indeed soon after weaning, Kobe had castrated the young bulls and nursed them in seclusion. He had raised them up to understand that all others were potential enemies and that he was the only friend to whom they should pledge allegiance. To them his words were law.

Secluded upbringing and castration of the young bulls was Kobe's own creation, based on his own experience as a young bull. He had been banished from the herd by another male after a fight over territorial rights and headship of the herd. For months he had lingered around the forest in isolation, till one lucky day he came across another herd of elephants whose master had just been killed by poachers. He wasted no time and immediately assumed authority. Not wanting rivals in his newly found kingdom, he decided to castrate all newly born bulls. That way he was certain no further power rivalries would arise. Yet he remained apprehensive of the other herds where the young bulls were not castrated. He had to find a way of introducing the same practice everywhere, and the only way of doing this was by training some of the castrated to fight to protect him. Besides they would be his instruments towards the enforcement of the law of castration.

Soon he was able to amass an army of demasculinised bull elephants. They performed their duty scrupulously well and for that reason were code-named 'Special Squad'. Kobe they referred to as director.

Many elephants especially those who had had an unfortunate experience in the hands of the special squad had turned up for the meeting out of fear. They knew very well that failure to turn up to Kobe's functions meant torture in the hands of the special squad.

As Kobe mounted the pavilion to address the mammoth group of beasts, the members of the special squad whose duty was to see to the security, lay camouflaged in the undergrowth at the perimeter of the meeting ground. Occasionally they could be glimpsed as they strolled around.

"Brethren", Kobe begun his address. "Never in the Ituri history, have elephants turned up to a meeting in such large numbers as we witness today. It makes me proud." He made a lengthy introduction to welcome all those present to the meeting. Kobe had one peculiarity that others hated. Throughout his introductory speech he appealed to facts of history of which none were conversant and in which many had no interest.

"My friends, in my lifetime I have been lucky to visit other animal kingdoms and learn from them", he continued with enthusiasm. "After careful study and speculation I have discovered that we are nothing compared to others. He went on to elaborate the difference with well researched statistics. Then he stood silent and stared at the speechless throng, wondering how much of the graceful words he spoke they had understood. Suddenly, in a low whisper-like tone he resumed. "Backward! That is the term to describe the present state of the elephant kingdom. Progressive! Developed! That describes others."

Full of emotion he went on to say: "If we want to get out of this plight, we can. All we need to do is to recognise our rights and duties like all other animals do. For that we need a constitution. We need law. We need it urgently." He paused letting his mind wander a little to how soon it would be before he bore full control of the entire elephant kingdom.

"Let me draw your attention to the rights we are ignorant of. This forest is our home. We are born here and most of us will die here. But look at how we view it! As a strange land. So strange that we can watch those two-legged creatures called men destroy it in whatever way they choose. What shall remain of our habitat, if all we do is sit and watch these things happen? I will tell you the answer. We shall be left with bare soil, meanwhile man will establish his own home here.

We had clean rivers where our ancestors drunk from, our heritage from which we too drunk. We also swam and wallowed there freely. What has become of them now?" Kobe pointed his trunk into space to show his smile. He seemed to forget that it was a meaningless venture given the hour of night in the forest. "Man has spoiled them. He makes our rivers teem with pungent human and industrial refuse. Meanwhile, foolish elephants look on. To drink, poor elephants have to walk for miles in search for clean water. And if one tries to get into what used to be clean water, well, if one is lucky one will emerge with a terribly unpleasant odour. Otherwise they perish as the water burns the insides forcing the heart to stop beating.

"Man is too clever for us. He wants to exterminate us from all angles. Even the air we breathe in is full of man's aerial disposables. We have to do something. We have to fight and defeat that clever being called man. United we can beat him." Once again, he gestured his trunk towards the skies as he contemplated his next sentence. "We have to fight man. I am talking about fighting to win. From my experience, the battle is easier if we have our own binding constitution." Again his eyes glared above everyone present making them feel they were being watched.

"One more example of how these men attack us. They kill us not for food but for our tusks. See for yourselves how they take advantage of us! How sad! Out of ignorance of our rights we are being wiped off the face of the earth. It makes me wonder as to how many here present know that it is our birth right to live to a ripe old age." There was tense silence as even those elephants who had previously closed their ears to whatever went on started to meditate on the truth that all have to die of old age.

"Friends, until we do something we shall continue dying. We are an endangered species near extinction, and unless we have our own law and constitution, we are all doomed. One by one, slowly but surely, man will finish us.

"I called this meeting so that we could draw an interim constitution to guide us until a chosen committee comes up with another. We need a constitution if we are to survive the human onslaught. And yet before we think of one we need a leader to guide us through this noble task."

From the audience came a murmur. Kobe's observed it. Well that was the impression he gave to others. "Let's not murmur. If anyone has something to say, say it out loud for the benefit of everyone. Murmuring is a sign of backwardness and it is precisely what we want to get rid of', Kobe explained.

"We were wondering as to why we should look for another leader when you are there: wise and capable as ever", came a voice hidden in the crowd.

"I hear you but there is a problem in your statement. You are one and yet you make reference to the word we. When did you have such a meeting so as to arrive to such a conclusion?"

He had hardly completed his statement when chanting came through the audience. It started with a few but soon spread across everywhere: "You are the chosen one, our king." The chorus rang through the peaceful quiet of the forest. Kobe enjoyed every bit of it. He let them chant while deep within he savoured the joy of having pushed through his idea unopposed. Indeed, long before the convention, Kobe and the Special Squad had everything laid out. Kobe was meant to be king come what may. They had even drafted the constitution. All that awaited was an opportunity to ratify it. Tonight was going to be the night to do this.

After a feeble protest, Kobe eventually accepted the appointment. He made no electoral speech but instead mobilised all elephants into small groups to draft the constitution. He scattered the members of the Special Squad among the groups. Their task was to push through the already drafted constitution. As for Kobe, he had no particular group that he was attached to. Instead, he went from one group to another making his contribution whenever he thought it was needed.

For days and nights the elephants busied themselves with discussions hardly excusing themselves except to eat and to perform other basic functions. Amidst them, the enthusiastic members of the Special Squad stressed their views and most of the time dominating the discussion. The frustrated majority, having reached tipping point and unable to comprehend anything sat and just watched things happen. In fact they would have preferred to leave but dared not tempt fate in the hands of Kobe's tools.

Kobe as supreme supervisor continued to move round from group to group answering questions that arose. Of course since many feared him, his presence was an added threat. They would simply keep quiet praying only for the moment he moved to the next group.

After five days of deliberation, late in the night the entire group assembled under the ancient baobab tree once again to hear the closing debates. Sita, one of Kobe's closest allies read the abridged draft constitution. "All elephants are keepers of each other", he started. "That is the summary of our constitution." Then he went on to spell out everything that had been put together.

As Sita read the constitution, the bewildered beasts kept glancing at each other with foolish grins on their faces, amazed at how the document had come to be worded in exactly the same words as they had agreed. Was it some kind of divine intervention that their words had been taken per se? Somehow it did give them satisfaction to think that their points had been taken into account. What they did not know was that Kobe's representatives within the different groups had merely pushed through the already made constitution thus making it feel as though they had all come up with the same words.

After Kobe's final allocution, the elephants dispersed and wandered back to their rightful territories in the forest. As they thumped their way through the dewy dawn of the forest, they argued amongst themselves each claiming that their group's words had been taken in full.

Meanwhile Kobe and the Special Squad withdrew to celebrate their victory. The power was in their hands and they had the authority to see to it that no other being threatened it. Kobe did not trust his appointment and ratification of the constitution ensured his security. He wanted a firmer grip and so he decided to hold a private conference with the special squad.

Through rumbling low noises Kobe poured out his counsel. "Brethren, I would like to thank you for the great job and for having elected me. Yet you ought to know that ahead of us lies a big challenge. Do not take it for granted that those elephants will do what we want. They are a perverse lot. It is your duty and mine to correct that attitude. How to do it? You already know. Use your acquired abilities. Torture anyone who seems to threaten you. There is no other law than you. I, myself will handle any complaints that may arise making sure that they are buried deep in the undergrowth."

They retreated to celebrate their happy time. Soon songs praising Kobe were trumpeted through the air as more and more impromptu compositions came about. For some reason, the more they praised him, the more authority he dished out. "Yes, my friends, you must realise now that you have no mothers or sisters. You are like destitute little ones who must survive at all costs. Just bear in mind that with your strength and ability you can get everything. Yes you can be anything."

# Chapter 2

The Constitution of Survivors as it was called did not please the majority of the elephants. Many of them had not even had the chance to speak during the discussions, and as for those who did, their contributions had been ignored. In the beginning they did not seem to bother since Kobe had called the constitution an interim one. But after several months had elapsed without the appointment of a constitutional committee, it became clear that nothing of the sort would ever take place. Kobe was the sole leader and author of the constitution.

For weeks even the ordinary elephants speculated on the constitution and came to the conclusion that there had been some dirty game that Kobe had played on them. For, if they had sat in different groups as they did, how come every elephant claimed that all their words were used in the constitution? It couldn't have been a miracle, let alone coincidence. But no one dared to complain out of fear. Secretly, however, they concluded and correctly so, that there had been some prior secret election and constitution, and that the convention was merely an opportunity to promulgate what had already been decided by Kobe.

Many elephants chose not to do anything about it out of fear. Others did not see reason to justify the effort. They preferred to let things take their natural course.

Not so for the fiery cow elephant, Ngina. She took upon herself the task of raising an underground resistance. She visited one herd after another meeting other cows. Ngina capitalised especially on one clause of the constitution which provided for the submission of all the newly born bulls to the special squad. According to her, the constitution was very much against cow elephants in as far as it promoted actions that were contrary to the natural law of generation and procreation. "Very soon", she argued, "there will be so many cows that the already aging bulls may not be able to cope with the natural call to procreate. The increase would lead to inbreeding. Mutilating young bull elephants would put an end to the future of the elephants." She was passionate about her course reminding the mothers that there were flaws in the constitution. "With her tusk high in the air she was ready to trumpet so loud but recalled that it was an underground movement she was leading. "My dear sisters, Kobe told you at the convention that humans were the enemy. How come the constitution said very little about the subject? Kobe is endangering rather than protecting elephants. He is a selfish old bull who is not content with the knowledge that he has lived to a ripe old age. He is not interested in our future but rather in our extinction."

At the convention, Ngina herself was gestating. She had vowed to keep her baby regardless of the gender. She campaigned among other gestating mothers promoting what she called a new awareness program. In the end they formed an association which they called the Mothers Union.

The objectives of the Mothers Union were to save all newly born bulls from the savagery of the special squad; raise them in secret places until they could be led elsewhere outside the boundaries of the Ituri Forest. All the members were vowed to secrecy and to mutually assist each other.

Since Kobe's constitution had prohibited any formation of associations without the approval of the director and his council, Ngina and her team submitted a different manifesto. It stated that the Mothers Union was created to educate young mothers on how to raise their young and on how to protect themselves from poachers during gestation. Kobe endorsed it as a noble objective.

For months Ngina and the other cow elephants did their duty meticulously well. When a male was born to a member of the union, they hid it. They let non-members hand over their bulls to the special squad.

Ngina founder and leader of the Mothers Union enjoyed a special privilege by virtue of her birth. She belonged to a clan of spiritual mediums and therefore had the power to mediate with the spiritual world of the departed ancestors.

That privileged position in itself added weight to her words and earned her respect.

Now the Ituri Forest had several rivers running through it, some of which were considered sacred. As sanctity rules dictated, not every elephant could approach such rivers without incurring an ancestral spirit curse. Spiritual mediums and those for whom they interceded could do so without fear. Being a medium, Ngina seized the opportunity to use sacred grounds for her projects. In fact she alleged that the spirit were behind their endeavours.

Adjacent to one of those sacred rivers there was a giant rock. Inside the rock was a cave with several chambers large enough to accommodate twenty full size elephants at any given time. This was believed to be home to the forest spirits. Ngina made this a secret brooding place for the recently born bulls. Nursing mothers hid their baby bulls there until they were old enough to be led out of the forest to seek protection of other forests.

Ngina's turn to use the nursery cave came. There she spent several hours of the day nursing Billy her baby bull. She dedicated most of her time to training him on the art of using his senses to detect danger and working out how to protect himself. Young Billy soon mastered the art so well that he could even sense when the members of the special squad passed by.

Time and again, Ngina would tell her son how bad and unjust the Constitution of Survivors was. With time Billy grew to resent the constitution and learnt how urgently he needed to exit this forest. Every so often, he would ask his mother; "When am I going to leave this place?"

"My son, you will do so as soon as you learn to desire the unknown without trace of fear. Desire it furiously. For it is such desire that helps you on your way", she would explain.

"But mother, I am sure I can look after myself."

"I know you can. You have yet to learn to behold the unknown."

"What is the unknown and where is it?"

Ngina would smile before going over the same story she always told. "Far away in the unknown lies the land of glory, a land which bestows and protects its inhabitants' rights. I am talking about the freedom, justice and equality for all." She would study her son's eyes marvelling at how focused and attentive he was. "Before you set off to find that land, you will need to desire to be there more than anywhere else. En route you will meet all kinds of obstacles including the ones your mind manufactures. If your desire is weak, you will give up. How unfortunate a thing that would be! Yet such things always seem to happen when one is close to the destination. Strong desire and determination must be your buckler and shield ensuring your safety. Believe me if your desire is strong, you will never give up even when the going gets tough. Instead you will keep going. As the saying goes; "*When the going gets tough, the tough get going*". That is why you need to prepare."

Young Billy shifted his curiosity to dreamland wondering what it looked like. After a long pondering he asked his mother. "How did you know about that land, when all your life you have lived in this forest?"

Ngina had never anticipated such a question but she also knew that she had to try to answer it without betraying her ignorance. "What a brilliant question! The answer is simple. It is one of those lessons one gains with time. Observation shows it but few notice it. All events in the world have their antitheses within the same world. If there is goodness then there is evil somewhere. If there is sickness then there must be health. So then if we have this unfortunate situation in Ituri, it follows that somewhere there is a better one. One that can be said to be like Ituri without the problems we have. I don't know where that land is, but I am relying on you. I want you to find it. It is my duty to prepare you for it."

Billy looked resolutely at his mother. In his mind he started to hatch out plans for the world he only knew in his imagination. As he did so, he created vivid images of what he wanted. Sinking deep into his unconscious was the desire to desire the mysteries of the unknown.

Everyday Ngina would encourage her son to ask questions. She did her best always to answer them. After countless hours of discussion, she would teach Billy a few songs. She would whisper into his ears:

*"You will need songs on your way. Songs unravel mysterious strength in one and get rid of fatigue and nostalgia. You may be alone and far away from loved ones but sweet melodies make loved ones present. With songs you can be alone but never lonely. You must learn them."*

The secret training lasted for almost two years. Ngina had confidence in her son. She breathed on him her blessing. She knew that nothing would shake the desire within him, that desire to find glory land. She studied his eyes as she always did. His eyes shone with confidence. Deep within his heart lay the courage to go through any obstacle that came his way. Physically too, he was ready.

As Ngina watched her son, tears tickled by the eminent separation filled her eyes. Between sobs she managed a few words. "Billy my son, you are ready. I am proud of you. Go and find that land of glory. Things will not be easy but stick to your guns. Remember from now on you are on your own and your own master. You must never distrust yourself any more. Once you get started, let there be no turning back. Time and again emotions will come between you and your goals, do not listen to them unless they positively contribute to your efforts. Aim and work towards your goals."

"Mother, you have my word", Billy stated with balls of tears clouding his eyes.

"I know and I believe in your ability.'

Elsewhere in the forest, Kobe the Wise Elder, director and King of Elephants lay in his quarters, admiring the paraphernalia built around him by the Special Squad. Every passing day he felt his glory rise. The news of support by the Mothers Union fanned the flames of pride. He could not see any appropriate explanation rather the willingness on the part of the female elephants to be subservient. As always, to make sure that everything was going to plan, he summoned Sita his special advisor.

Sita came in and prostrated in an Ituri traditional salutation to a superior. Kobe watched with his usual smile of derision. With his trunk he signalled him to sit.

"Sita my friend, how nice to see you! Let us take stock of our progress so far", he said. "I am more interested in what we have achieved since the formation of the Constitution of Survivors. Have there been any casualties of any kind? Is there anyone you consider expendable?

"Sir director, Wise counsellor", Sita started, "so far nothing."

"That is good to know. I take it everything is going in our favour. The Mothers Union and the steady enrolments into the Special Squad is a sign of good work. Sita my faithful friend, it proves the point that our plan is working well. We are about to realise our dream."

"Yes, Your Excellency everything is splendid."

"Well of course, my wise counsel generates splendid results and for your information, more are in the pipeline", bemused Kobe.

Sita stooped his head low. He knew somewhere in the system things were not right and telling Kobe that was very difficult. He waited for the chance, and indeed it came when Kobe started to talk.

"What is wrong with you my faithful friend? Is there anything bothering you?"

"Well yes, but I trust You Highness has the answers to everything."

"Spit it out my faithful friend and I will deal with it. For as you indeed say, there is nothing that I cannot sort out", Kobe boasted. "I am the hero of Ituri and nothing surpasses my wisdom."

"Yes my Lord. It is about the number of enrolments to the special squad. I feel there is something wrong. The numbers are not proportionate to the females that were gestating and should have had their calves."

"Kobe laughed heartily while Sita gaped unamused. "Of course, that is expected. Some produce females and others males. Simple logic is all it takes to decipher the situation. So Sita my son, I am sure everything is under control."

"I agree. That may be true but there is something else". Sita rose to his feet. Over the years he had developed a habit of pacing around especial when confronted by what he construed to be a difficult problem. Somehow, whenever he did that even Kobe took him seriously.

"It seems to me some mothers are not reporting their young. I wouldn't be surprised if some of them are being smuggled out of Ituri Forest. To be frank, I think the Mothers Union is behind it. I do not trust them."

Kobe cast upon Sita one of those deadly looks of his. He did not say anything, but sort of concluded that it was in the nature of an emasculated bull to feel jealous and small before females, especially when their handicap was publicly known. In Kobe's mind, the Mothers Union was second to the Special Squad in servitude. He allowed himself to cool off before continuing. "Before you tamper with anything, I suggest you make a thorough investigation. As for now go and have the number of guard posts doubled."

Guard posts had been established shortly after the formation of the constitution. The special squad manned them day and night. In the name of the constitution, they had been expected to abandon guard whenever alarms were made. Sita went to carry out the orders he had been given. He left Kobe to think the matter over.

Kobe knew that, as leader the worst thing to do would be to frustrate those upon whom he depended. Now he was caught in a dilemma. He needed Sita and the special squad for defence. But he also needed the Mothers Union to assure continuity of the squad. Yet if what Sita said was true, then he would be forced to take action against the Mothers Union.

Again he thought of the guards stationed at the guard posts, who had authority to attack any intruders and to quell any subversive activities from within. If it were true then they would have reported it to him long before. He dismissed it as a mere speculation.

He tried to concentrate on the progress thus far but he could not. His mind went over the possibilities of what Sita said was happening. He started to talk to himself. "In that case, then I might be forced to think that both the Mothers Union and the special squad were guilty of negligence."

# Chapter 3

Mother and son were ready to set off together. Ngina, who knew the forest well, would lead the way, carefully avoiding all the guard posts. As usual the Mothers Union members were as involved as Ngina herself. They played the same trick that they had always worked well for them. One of the mothers, a union member had lain groaning pretending to be unwell. The news quickly spread and the emergency alarm trumpet was sounded. As expected, every squad member rushed in the scene leaving their guard posts unmanned. Ngina, taking advantage of the situation quickly led Billy out of the forest.

It was dawn when Ngina left Billy alone and returned to the forest. Billy, now a sturdy young bull set off on his way to the unknown. He relied entirely on what he had learnt from his mother and on his own volition. He was determined to find the land of glory if not for himself, at least for the sake of his mother. He was on his own en route to the unknown. His mother had always sung to him about it and now the time had come to use them. The lyrics flowed freely in his mind bringing alive the sweet memories of the times he spent with his mother. But she was not there to sing with him. He needed to get used to singing alone.

Billy glanced around his surroundings to make sure that no body was watching him. He took a deep breath and he was ready. He thumped his feet to rhythm and marching to tempo started to sing with closed eyes about the land he was out to find.

> The land of glory, the land of success
> Land of Glory where are you?
> The land of glory is everywhere
> Its direction and reality are
> Embedded upon the magic of
> Try-try trying …

Trying even when it seems hopeless
Try-try trying is its direction and key
The distance is dependent on
The zeal with which one try tries
Try-try trying …

The secret fare to glory land
That secret lies deep in my heart
The distance to glory land I know depends on
Try-try trying …

And so it was that Billy set off knowing that glory land was his destination and that trying and determination were the directions, distance and the vehicle to lead him there.

Billy planned his journey such that by day he hid in the undergrowth in the bushes and slept. At night he would walk and graze. He followed a stretch of greenery that spread northwest of the Ituri. How far the greenery stretched was not the question to ask. All he wanted was to find glory land. Fuelled by the hatred for the murderous tyrants in the Ituri Forest and encouraged by the desire to avenge his suffering not by fighting but being successful in life, he thumped on, on his way.

Billy was many miles away from the Ituri Forest when the sun rose. He hid between bushes and slowly drifted to sleep.

Ngina re-entered the forest just when the mock emergency was at its climax. Iba, the mother elephant at the centre of action lay down groaning and moaning surrounded by herds of elephants. Among them were the members of the special squad who had abandoned their guard posts in order to attend to the emergency.

Ngina pushed her way through. "Let the spiritual medium through", she trumpeted as she pushed her way. "Delivering an urgent message from the spirit world". She was soon face to face with Iba. A few gentle strokes and meaningful glances informed Iba that Billy was safely out of the forest. Almost immediately Iba stopped groaning. Ngina meanwhile continued taking charge of the situation. "The spirits have relented. She will live." Then she turned her attention to youthful members of special squad. "Come on! Let's help her to her feet. She needs some sleep. Any strong bulls willing to lend a trunk?" she rumbled. "You over there", she pointed to a young member of the special squad, "come and help the poor old girl."

The other elephants watched with great admiration how Ngina had solved the problem. It was like a miracle to them. Others attributed that miraculous display to the spirits that worked through her. The same action however, did raise some questions from some members of the Special Squad who wondered why she had rarely been seen or active in the last twenty four months. They knew she was alive and about somewhere but nobody really understood what she had been up to. To make matters worse, she had arrived late to the scene of emergency. Even without solid evidence, Sita who had been investigating the Mothers Union was more than happy to conclude that Ngina was involved in some underground activity. He left the rest and headed straight for Kobe's quarters.

Ignoring the traditional salutation protocol, Sita burst in. "My Lord King ..."

Kobe did not take it kindly. He cut in. "Ah, ah! That is not the way my faithful friend. You know the protocol. Everyone prostrates before their king."

"I am terribly sorry, Your Highness", said Sita trying very much to hide his anger and frustration.

Kobe was in no rush. "Saying sorry in itself is not enough. You have to do what you are supposed to do before your superior", Kobe grunted. "Do it now before Kobe strips you off the little honour and title", he commanded.

Sita felt not so much frightened as humiliated and angry. He thought of the respect he commanded from other elephants as a result of the position he held and started to imagine how losing his power would feel. He even saw himself being kicked about by the Special Squad. With sweat dripping at the tip of his trunk he did what he had to do. He fell down prostrate as was expected.

"That is more like it", yapped Kobe. "Now you can arise and proceed to say whatever you were in a rush to say. I am all ears."

Still angry at what he thought was belittling correction, Sita got up. He paced about briefly. "My Lord, I have to conclude that Ngina and the Mothers Squad may have something to do with the depleting number of bulls being recruited into the squad."

"I am all ears", Kobe frowned.

"Ngina has not been around for quite a long time. Well she has but made next to no public appearances at all. I guess the word here is scarce. She was scarce. She was very rarely seen." He paced about with his little frisky tail up in the air. "Today, she did emerge in public. Yes, she did. But she was very late. As My Lord knows the constitution dictates that all elephants must respond to an emergency without exception. Where was she? Why did she come late? I know the answer. She was taking advantage of the unmanned guard posts. She was leading her team of bulls out of the forest. Her secret brood of bulls intended to overthrow you perhaps." Sita knew he had thrown his bomb. He paced up and about waiting for the impact to sink in. Deep within he knew whether Ngina was guilty or not he would have to do something to pin her down. He resumed his talk with questions intended to help him build his case.

"If my master, the king does not mind then I will ask him one or two silly questions. I must of course emphasise that, My Lord the King, is in no way compelled to answer them. But at least he can think over them."

With his trunk erect in the air, Kobe signalled for Sita to continue. Already by now his mind was working full speed questioning as to how if he had an efficient squad, they had failed to detect such alleged breach of the constitution.

Sita went on. "Well, master. You are the only bull in service. I mean fully functional in all aspects since all the others have been reproductively emasculated including me."

"Stop beating about the bush. Come to the point. I have other things to worry about", yelled Kobe.

"Yes sir. My point is that I am sure you know which cows you serviced and when."

"I didn't know that I was supposed to keep record. Let's say I do remember who though not necessarily when. What is your point?"

"When did you last service, Ngina?"

Kobe looked up as he tried to appeal to his powers of recall. There was nothing he could associate it with. He felt lethal dose of anger stream through his blood. He gnashed his gums in rage as he realised he had never touched Ngina. "I have never", he answered in a soft voice.

"Then shall I say our medium friend is guilty of avoiding my Lord the King of Ituri elephant kingdom?"

Sita's answer angered Kobe the self-made king. He thumped his feet aimlessly and grunted so loud that even Sita was scared. "There is no room for traitors in the elephant kingdom. I want every piece of information about her. Follow her wherever she goes. I want to know what she had been up to in the last four years. Leave no stone unturned."

"Yes sir. Everything shall be carried out as you command", affirmed Sita. He just could not hide his eagerness. "I will have it carried out at once. I shall even have all members of the Mothers Union rounded up and interrogated. If they refuse to cooperate, they shall be tortured until they reveal everything they had been doing." He stopped talking and started to pace up and down as he always did when something was troubling him.

"What now?" Kobe asked.

"Allow me ask one more question."

"Go right ahead."

Sita cleared his voice and couldn't be bothered to excuse himself. "If I recall correctly, during the convention to draw the constitution, Ngina was gestating. Whose seed was she carrying if it was not yours?" This time he did not wait for the answer. He bowed and made for the exit glad that he had put Kobe in a state of mind that would force him to back his action.

Indeed Sita had angered Kobe. He once again grunted so loudly that Sita who was by now heading towards the guard post retraced his steps in haste. He prostrated as expected and started to speak. "Is anything the matter with his Lordship the king?"

Kobe who by now had mellowed down stood both trunk and tail erect. "Everything is absolutely fine."

"Very well then my Lord, I shall make exit for I have work to do", stated Sita.

"Make it quick and thorough. I mean waste her if you have to", Kobe called after Sita.

Sita was soon down the gate surrounded by his handpicked members of the squad. "We have a few fat butts to kick. The worthless cows of the worthless Mothers Union have been plotting to overthrow us. As they say cut off the head and the rest of the body will fall useless. Start with Ngina. As for the rest, make them feel the pain."

The troops were soon on their mission to hunt down and terrorise each and every members of the Mothers Union. Sita and two others went for Ngina.

Sensing that something was wrong, Ngina marched out to meet them. "What have I done to deserve an honourable visit from chief Sita? Please do make yourselves comfortable." She stretched her trunk. "Is there anything I can do for you?" she asked.

Sita had not expected any questions. His plan had been to have her beaten and then arrested. Now face to face with her, he saw she was not at all afraid of them and more so she wore a happy face. He wondered if that joy and confidence in her meant she was innocent or merely using it to cover her guilt. As he watched on in silence, Ngina continued to talk. "Could it be that the masters of the forest have finally remembered ancestors and want mediation?

This particular question confused Sita even more. It also added some fear into his anger. He realised he was going to be doing what was considered not just sacrilege but also impossible. Who was he to arrest a medium? Never before, had it been done. And yet for the sake of the new order they were creating, it was necessary to do so especially if the medium's actions were contrary to the constitution. He raised his right foot to command silence. "Me and my assistants would like to ask you some questions about the Mothers Union."

"I am at you service", replied Ngina. Her attention was drawn to several young members of the Mothers Union who were larking about as though they had a message for her. She tried to use eye signals but they persisted.

Sita was now pacing about as he spoke his guards took their positions. "Before I say anything on the subject I want you to realise that it is a serious matter for which I will not accept lies. I want the whole truth."

"I will be glad to tell you the whole truth if I am allowed."

Sita embarked on his question. He started with simple facts about the Mothers Union and reached the climax when he resorted to some personal questions about Ngina's whereabouts in the recent past. All along she had fearlessly answered his questions in such a way that could easily be construed as arrogance. Sita tried to threaten her but she was not moved. At one point he had his guards beat her up before he resumed.

"Tell me the truth. We know you formed the union for the sole purpose of smuggling young bulls out of the forest. I know that is why you have been scarce here."

"What then do you want me to say? Your statement seems to be your conclusion as well. What difference would it make if I affirm or deny it?" retorted Ngina with force.

"You have the choice to make, to tell the truth and save the Mothers Union or to keep quiet and have my team wipe out the entire lot", fumed Sita.

Ngina knew the special squad could do anything they wanted. She would rather die alone, after all her little Billy was far gone. It was for his sake that she had worked hard to form the union. But now that he was gone it would not be right for her to let the mothers face death. She would have to face it alone if that would help the rest. She spoke out. "Promise me that you will not harm the other members if I tell you the truth," she requested.

"I cannot promise that since at the very moment some of them might be subjected to some pain. I mean, if they have not yet cooperated. Of course, if you do as I say I can always call off any action against them" Sita explained.

"Then have it done now. Send one of your friends now. As soon as he comes back with assurance, only then can I begin my story."

Sita and his guards exchanged whispers after which one rose to go. Ngina looked at him but she was far from talking. She was planning to make her interrogation something for others to learn from. She was thinking of having it in front of the entire elephant community of Ituri. She looked at Sita and smiled. "Since your friend has gone maybe I shall tell you something of interest. I gave birth not so long ago to a young bull. I couldn't stand the thought of having him mutilated by guys with misguided ideologies. I thought of killing him but the maternal instinct forbade me. That is when I decided to lead him out of the forest. I left him to go out somewhere else where he can start a new life."

Sita fumed. "Are you aware of the gravity of the crime you have committed?"

"My conscience tells me otherwise. Indeed anyone interested in the welfare of elephants will tell you that we are going about it the wrong way." She whisked her tail. "By the way councillor, I do not intend to answer any of your questions without others present. I stood for the union and it is my wish to be interrogated with all of them present. Do include Kobe as well, for he deserves to hear everything too."

Once again Sita was caught off guard. "But that would …" he started but was rudely interrupted.

"I do not take your buts", she broke in just as Sita began to speak and continued. "If you want me to speak or answer any questions I want the rest of the mothers to be there. I mean what I have said". She sat down silent.

"I am afraid if that is the case we shall have you arrested here now. Come on! Compatriots arrest her."

They led Ngina to the detention camp that was established by the special squad. It was known that whoever went there never returned alive. She was detained in isolation from the other mothers who had already been arrested. From time to time they would bring her out of the cell to watch mothers from the union being tortured. Ngina would only wave her trunk to encourage them.

When in the morning Ngina was summoned before the interrogation team. She was marched with her team to the constitution meeting grounds where only loyal Kobe followers had assembled. As Ngina was the key witness and all the questions were addressed to her. "Ngina will you please tell us about the Mothers Union", Sita asked.

She was on the pedestal where everyone could see. "What is there to tell you? The only thing to put forth is that the Mothers Union is there to struggle for the survival of the endangered species. We wanted to save the elephants."

"Tell us about your members", Sita demanded in an increasingly forceful voice.

"Nothing special about them, they are just elephants like anybody else. The only difference is their determination to stand for the truth. And I believe our future depends on our ability to promote the truth."

"What sort of truth?" Sita interjected.

Ngina smiled and went on to divert the interrogation to herself. "You want to know the truth? You will and here is the truth. I gave birth to a handsome bull, kept and taught him in seclusion for two years. He left the forest not so long ago and I am proud of that. I helped him because I believe it is against the rights of elephants to be mutilated. I am sure if that was what Mother Nature wanted all bulls would have been born in that state. There would never have been such a thing as others claiming that they know what is right for everyone else."

Sita pushed on with the questioning. "Do you realise that by so doing you are violating the constitution which so to say is the voice of the rest of the elephant community?"

"Sorry, I have never really acknowledged that constitution you talk about. Much as I know it is a tool of oppression and dominance. Ask yourself, if you were born with rights which should be first?" She stared at Sita in the eye. "I am sure councillor Sita does not know the answer. I will help him. In my opinion, the first should be the right to be elephants. That right to be male or female without anyone else trying to interfere, is what I am talking about. Castration is a clear violation of that right."

Sita felt the speech was being directed to him. He wanted to have the whole issue concluded. "I am going to have to close this meeting in a few minutes. As for Ngina, she already knows that she is guilty…"

Ngina broke in cutting him short. "I am guilty of doing the right thing. You know it but simply refuse to admit it." She paused to smile at the rest of the union members who paid close attention to the whole interrogation. They smiled back as she resumed. "Maybe you are truly ignorant. May be you do not know the truth. Maybe your boss has been successful in making idiots out of you."

Her response infuriated Sita. He concluded in his mind that she had to die for it. He tried to contain himself but he just could not. For her part, Ngina was just getting into the mood to talk. "I have tried to help other mothers to see the light by telling them that Kobe and his plans are but a means to the extinction of the elephant kingdom. Yes I did and I am glad to have done so. I managed to get a few young bulls out. Wherever they go, I am sure they will be working to ensure survival of our kind."

"You despicable creature! You have betrayed the entire kingdom. You will answer for it before the entire assembly of elephants", Sita fumed.

"I will only be too happy to do so and pray that such an opportunity will help others see the truth."

Sita had had enough. He stormed out in rage and headed straight to Kobe to report his findings. As was expected Kobe summoned all elephants to a meeting. There in front of every elephant present the charges against her were read. Sita took to the podium.

"Ngina founder of the rebel group, she defies the law and the constitution and goes on to keep an army of bulls whose whereabouts is yet to be established. She is guilty of betraying the entire elephant kingdom…" The accusations which were not written anywhere but simply related at whim lasted about half an hour.

As Sita the prosecutor poured out his accusations, Ngina marvelled with such joy that none who awaited execution could ever afford. She thought of young Billy on his way to the unknown land and the feeling of pride filled her heart. She knew that even if she died her son was safe somewhere. She smiled at everyone happily giving them trunks up. Her followers and sympathisers meanwhile wept for her.

At the end of the accusation narrative Kobe stood to address the gathering. "So far as I am concerned that traitor should never be allowed to speak. She is a total disgrace who wants to poison others with her words. The only place for her is the pit of destruction. Take her there to await death. Let her die with disgrace. "As for each and every one of you, let this be a lesson. Anyone who will follow in her footsteps will receive the same treatment. They shall be annihilated." With that Kobe the King of the Ituri elephants, the Director and Wise Councillor stormed out of the meeting place leaving Ngina in the hands of the special squad. The pit of destruction was her destiny.

Execution by throwing in a pit was Kobe's invention and had been used to secretly dispose of those deemed to be threats to the special squad. Ngina became the first to be publicly thrown into the pit to be left to starve to death. A guard was mounted at the mouth of the pit to ensure that no body brought her any food.

Ten days later Ngina died of starvation. The guard was promptly removed. Kobe and indeed his closest allies were relieved though only temporary. In mind Kobe was disturbed. He could not stop questioning how his trusted squad had been outwitted by a simple cow. He withdrew with his close pal Sita. Together they decided to amend the constitution. From thence no elephant would be allowed to form any kind of association and no one who wanted to leave the forest could do so without permission directly from Kobe. And if one was to leave the forest, it had to be done so via recommended routes only. All gestating cows were to be kept under guard twenty four seven.

# Chapter 4

On the night Ngina died, Billy who had camped and slept under a cool tree dreamt about her being trapped in a deep and narrow pit. She was dying but managed to talk to him; "Billy my son", she had said. "I am going to die but do not worry about me. Simply walk on, and do not look back. I can see you are about to make it."

Billy had woken up expecting to find her but she was nowhere. It was merely a dream about the reality which though he did not know about had actually taken place. He reminded himself that he was alone and would be so for as long as the trek took.

The sun was not overhead but it was extremely hot. Billy looked from side to side and spun round to make sure everything was okay. A stone throw away he could see heaps of sand rising like mountains. Clouds of dust rose as winds whirled round as though navigating their way through the mountains of sand. Billy did not know where he was. He wondered why his mother had not mentioned this kind of phenomenon. Even the greenery that he had followed for days was no longer as green. Brown dust covered the leaves and the trees were not that tall. As he manoeuvred his way through torrents of dust poured on his back, sometimes catching and irritating his tiny eyes. He was thirsty but there was no immediate sign of water. As he meandered behind another sand mountain his eyes locked on to an unexpected view a pool of water. He ran into it ignoring the possible danger of an enemy or the unknown. He drank his fill and thereafter dived into water to allow its coolness to rejuvenate his aching muscles. He wallowed and rolled over and over; and with his trunk blew into the air sprays of water.

A few metres away, Madji the camel was hurrying to the same pool to replenish his depleting body water reservoir before continuing on the long journey across the desert. Much to his surprise a strange creature lay wallowing about in the water. Mindful of his own safety Madji stopped to watch.

From his sojourns across the desert to different cities Madji thought he knew what the creature was. It was just like the ones he had seen performing in the circus. As to what the creature was doing far away from the city, he just could not understand. He dismissed the ideas and started to focus on how uncouth and disrespectful the creature must be, to soak its filthy body in the drinking waterhole.

The animal meanwhile remained in the water enjoying itself. Madji moved nervously closer to acquire a good look. As he approached the creature suddenly looked up. Their fear-written eyes locked on to each other as underneath their hides, each harboured fear of the other. Madji broke the silence. 'I mean no harm, pal whoever you are.'

'Me too', responded Billy happy to be able to steal a lungful of the much needed oxygen after several minutes of holding his breath. 'I am Billy the Elephant. Yes I am an elephant from Ituri forest'. He lifted his trunk to reveal a large mouth in what Madji interpreted as the creature's smile.

Parting the ropes that hung over his lips, Madji responded in kind. 'Call me Madji the Camel. I spend my life slaving for the two-legged creatures, the humans. I trek back and forth across these desert sands ferrying humans and their merchandise on my back.'

Billy, now out of the water and unable to hide his surprise looked hard at Madji. Much as he knew and even his mother had told him so, all humans were bad. They killed animals. He looked at Madji's tall, heavy harp-shaped body suspended on long, tough legs which made him look like some sort of unstable and clumsy being. He kept wondering what was so special about him that he worked for humans and yet remained unharmed. The more he cogitated about it the more he questioned why he could not do the same. Moreover, with his stout build he could easily be of better advantage than the clumsy creature before him.

Madji who had been studying his friend spoke up in a lowly voice. 'May I ask why my friend is not only looking surprised but also lost in thought?'

'Nothing special', replied Billy. 'I was just wondering how you manage to live with men when we elephants fear them. As a matter of fact because of them I am fleeing my home.' Billy did not tell the whole story about the Constitution of Survivors. What he said was just enough for Madji.

'Well some humans are really bad, but others are good', started Madji. Then just as Billy was getting ready to hear more he changed the topic. 'I am rather thirsty. If you don't mind, I will have my drink now.'

'Of course, I don't. Please go right ahead', Billy said as he stepped out of the water. 'I will wait here for you.'

The wait seemed forever as Madji filled his reservoir in anticipation for a long trek ahead. Billy meanwhile imagined a world where he would be one with humans until such a time when he would return to tell his relatives about it. He closed his tiny eyes as visualised everything. Unfortunately the process was cut short when, with a mighty grunt Madji announced his availability.

'That was a nice drink. Now my system is as good as new. Anyway, as I was saying some humans are kind to animals.'

Billy spoke with enthusiasm. 'Then let me come with you so that I too may work for humans. I am sure your boss likes animals.' He looked at Madji but did not give the other chance to speak. All he wanted was a chance to start his life all over again. 'Friend let me come with you. I am prepared to do anything to ensure my survival.'

'I wish it was as easy as that', Madji remarked.

With a horrified look, Madji lowered his body down. By now Billy was rambling on. 'By the way, where exactly are you going? Is it near here?'

'Got to go across the desert, about four days and nights walk away. There is a big market place where humans meet to exchange different goods. I am taking the load you see there on my back to my owner.'

Billy looked at Madji's back just behind the hump and at the load on it. At the sides resting on his body, two loads balanced. Until now, he had just thought of it as part of Madji's body. He could not imagine how it felt but he thought it was not such a bad thing otherwise Madji would have been moaning about it. Somehow at the back of his mind he couldn't help wondering how he coped with the journey. 'If you don't mind me asking, doesn't your master worry about you travelling all by yourself?'

'He probably doesn't. Personally, I am used to it. I take my time and follow other camels across the desert. For some reason, the people know who I belong to and don't even bother me.'

'They must respect your master', Billy commented.

'I think fear is the right word. He can be ruthless when he means to be. I am told that he once went through the entire journey killing at least one person in every household because someone had made off with some load from his camel. From thence, no body messes with his camels. In short that is why I often travel alone.'

'Out of curiosity how does your owner get to the market place?'

'Sometimes he rides on a camel but most of the time he uses the air sailing machine called aeroplane. That sailing machine is known to cover the entire route in a matter of hours.'

Poor Billy! He had never heard of aeroplanes. As for humans, his knowledge was purely based upon hearsay. Now here he stood before some unusual looking beast that knew and worked for men, and spoke of the flying gadgets that humans made for themselves. The whole idea of flying gizmos was strange. To the best of his knowledge the only flying creatures he knew were either insects or birds. He smiled in his blissful ignorance then asked: 'What do aeroplanes look like?'

'I have never been close to one but I know they are not like birds or insects that fly by flapping their wings. These are mankind's creature. They fly in the sky with roaring noise. It is just as though thunder was following them and sometimes they leave behind in the sky a trail of their paths.'

'Humans must be wonderful creatures, sailing in the air. How I wish I could be like you privileged to be with humans!'

As Madji spoke, Billy listened with admiration and all the attention he could give. This beast knew a lot. He even explained why humans hunted and killed elephants. 'Sad to say but it is the truth. Elephants are not usually killed for food. They are killed for their tusks.' Billy started to wonder whether that is what humans did at Ituri.'

'Elephant tusks', Madji went on, 'are highly valued by humans and from them different things can be made: cups, plates and dagger-sheaths for the sons of the wealthy.'

'What are those things you are talking about?' yapped Billy.

'It is difficult to explain but one day you will see them. Humans use cups to drink with and plates to serve their food. Dagger sheaths are used to keep sharp knives.' He looked at Billy wondering how much of his explanation he understood. 'Any way friend, it is not a good idea for you to seek sanctuary where I go. Those men will rejoice in killing you. They might even call it some kind of divine providence.'

Billy was angry but just as he was heating up with hatred for humans Madji introduced another story. 'Even my own life has its end but I prefer not to think about it. I know that when I become old, and unable to do as much as I do now, man will slaughter me for food. That is the ultimate end but does not eliminate the unexpected demise when some human being decides to take their frustration on you. Yes, for no reason at all you end up being gunned down.' Rather that imbuing him with courage, Madji's talk was instead making Billy angry and afraid. 'Knowing what man is capable of doing to me does not discourage me in any way.

I know I have to live as long as I am able to and to the best of my ability.' Madji turned his eyes to Billy. 'To you my friend I should say, do not think very much of the dangers that might come your way. Think rather of the few minutes or hours of happiness that you can have.'

Billy cocked his big ears. 'I am not even sure whether I can ever have such a time in my life.'

'Anyway my friend, what I want to say is that you still have chances around. I have seen elephants work in the circus. They get smacked here and there but they are alive. Best of it all, their food is assured.' Madji in his travels had had vast experiences and had also learnt a lot. Much as he knew about the circus, he could not exactly remember where about it was. He turned to the story he had once heard. 'An acquaintance once told me about a place far away from here, where elephants work for humans.'

'What did you just say?' queried Billy.

'India. That is the name of that place where man and elephant work together', continued Madji. 'Who knows may be one day you will find yourself in such a situation! All it takes is self-discipline. They use you for their purposes in return for the food you need.'

'At this point I am prepared to try anything provided my safety and happiness are assured', retorted Billy.

'Sounds good, that principle of yours. I pray you stick to it.' Madji started to prepare to get up in order to continue on his journey.

'But where exactly is the place you talk about? How does one get there?'

'I have heard about it but I don't know where it is', Madji answered. 'In short, I don't know where it is but somehow I have the feeling that you will find it. All I can say is walk on. Do not stray far off the greenery for the moment you do so the hot desert sun and sands will roast you.' He glanced over his body and then back at Billy. 'You see my skin is designed for hardship and service in these areas. Its tough texture enables me to go through the desert sun without losing much water. Besides, we camels can stay several days without food. Yes', he said proudly. 'We camels are the kings of the desert and the only reliable transport for many.' He grinned briefly. 'As I was saying, if you keep to the greenery I should think that someday you will find a home.'

Madji rose up making sure that his baggage balanced safely and walked back into the water. 'A bit more for the road', he said as he lowered his neck into the water hole once again. The time he took was just incredible given that, not so long back had had a drink. Billy stared on as he pondered his next action.

Madji the Camel finally left the waterhole to resume his conversation. 'As I was saying, walk on along the greenery. I have heard rumours of a miracle world which lies at the end of that greenery. They say that at times it is full of green grass and trees and water. At other times it is said to fill with some magical cold white powder. While other creatures hide away from the cold magic, the children of man rejoice playing with the powder. They are said to build rounded shapes which look like humans.'

'If I should copy you well, you are kind of saying that I am heading to a place where I will freeze my massive heap of flesh?'

'Cold is not really a problem, one can always adapt to it. I should imagine it very different from the sands and heat that cover the territories I dwell in where one has to be highly suited to survive.' He glanced Billy's way and could just about anticipate what he was going to say. He countered it. 'Now go on your way. I don't want you getting ideas. My world is very hostile and I wouldn't recommend it even to my worst enemy. Go along the greenery and may Allah go with you'.

'I am sorry but who is Allah?'

'Allah is the greatest power conceivable. It is said to help creatures in need. My master says that he is the creator of all that is', Madji explained.

'Whoever Allah is, let him not be a human and if he be one he damn be different from, and better than the ones I have heard about.' Billy did not hide his sarcasm.

Madji ignored it. 'And one more thing friend, as you go remember in this part of the world, there is no taking things for granted. Never for a moment assume that it is safe simply because it is quiet. Have room for doubt, in that way if the worst comes you shall not be disappointed'.

Madji went his way and Billy too. In a fortnight Madji would retrace his steps across the same desert. As for Billy, nothing was certain. He was out to find the Land of Glory. Whatever it cost and wherever it was, did not matter. The desire in him would only be satisfied when he got there. He thanked Madji for enlightening him and bringing him face to face with the world and its wonders.

The encounter with Madji had made a very deep impression on Billy. Even a week after they had parted at the pool, the incident remained vivid in his mind and affected all his actions. He thumped his way through half-minded and lazily too. Then plagued by fatigue and pained by memories of his mother and Madji, he stopped and stood still. His mind retired to a retrospective journey over events with the elephants in the Ituri Forest. He tried to imagine how the young bulls who had succumbed to Kobe's castration fared. A negative inner voice crawled in and made its opinion known. 'Oh yes, they are better than you a mere vagabond who depends on unknown motivation.'

He wondered what the dream about his mother had meant. Was she truly dead? He did not dismiss it. He merely left it as a possibility. He missed her then and wished he too were dead. He recalled his mother's admonition: "It is better and indeed more honourable to die trying than to die giving up."

Somehow he started to feel different as his face blossomed in an unexplained smile. With untold happiness his mind shifted concentration on Madji and his world of desert sand and yet he remained a happy beast.

He thought of the world ahead of him and imagined himself exposed to chances similar to Madji's full knowledge of the world. He smiled at the thought wondering how nice it would be to return one day to the Ituri Forest and relate his story to the rest, enlighten the ignorant and broaden their views. Again a spasm of nostalgic feelings streamed into his blood. It was then that he decided to hum the songs his mother had taught him, one after another. Finally he came to his favourite and decided to sing out loud accompanying it with feet thumping:

> Somewhere in glory land,
> all, their home shall find
> Full of everything judged by
> Equal rights and justice.
>
> Glory land, Glory land
> Everybody sings and desires
> Yet none knows the way or
> Direction and distance
>
> The wise! They say
> it is as near as it is far
> Far but can be near
>
> The key, the key to Glory land
> The key daily is sung by everyone
> Try, try, trying
> through thick and thin
> Follow your dreams, act your dreams
> And soon you will be there
> Try, try, trying ...

Billy felt renewed in spirit and began to walk again. After about an hour he climbed a sand dune and stared at the horizon. The narrow strip of greenery he had followed seemed to turn into forest, though not as big as Ituri. He smiled with the biggest stretch of lips he could afford and sighed in relief. 'I have made it', he started to talk. 'That is Glory Land', he told himself. 'One more hour and I will be there.'

He looked at the direction from where he came and said out loud: 'Thanks Madji my good friend. I may never see you again but as long as I live I will never forget you. Ituri needs guys like you to bail them out of their ignorance. I tell you friend, there is a lot of ignorance there. Imagine how they are endangering the already endangered species by performing acts which they think will save them.'

About the same time Madji the camel who was on his way back from the market, stopped at the same pool he had met with Billy. He lay down and let memories of Billy become alive in him. Then he spoke out loud: 'Billy mate, I admire your courage. Never before have I met someone who probed the unknown with a determination like yours. Allah will see you safely to your destination.'

# Chapter 5

As Billy drew closer to his destination, his nerves went out of control. Balls of sweat formed on the bare parts of his body. His heart pounded twice as fast, and as loud as an ancient royal funeral drum. Several times he would inhale and exhale large amounts of air, letting it out as he repeated the word "Relax". The magic was not working. He was uncontrollably anxious and even the gracious words he had rehearsed vanished leaving him empty handed. He decided he would face things as they came but first he would find himself place to rest. He found himself once again on the crest of the hill looking back at the direction of the Ituri Forest and comparing the Ituri to the forest ahead he embarked on his self talk. 'Behind lies a land of threats and danger to many and ahead stands a vast expanse of the unknown. Either way life is uncertain but liveable.'

Billy entered Skuna Forest shortly after sunrise. He had been walking every night for well over two months. He made a careful survey of the place with all his senses on the alert. He passed what he thought was a dry tree glad to have something to rub his skin on. Much to his surprise the tree fell to the ground. He stared at the strange branch which was no way like the ones he knew. Had it fallen because termites had eaten up the roots or was that their nature? He wondered. 'I would better refrain from leaning on anything until I have learnt more about them', he told himself. He raised his trunk to sniff the air. He could not detect any signs of danger so he chose a place by the water to hide and sleep.

What Billy did not know was that he had camped on forbidden territory. Being unlettered, he had ignored the signposted messages. Right above where he lay stood the sign in red ink: "PRIVATE PROPERTY; TRESPASSERS WILL BE PROSECUTED".

He lay enjoying the cool of the forest and the breeze from the pool. Billy tried to avoid sleep so as to study what went on in the area.

Late in the afternoon Billy was awakened from his day dreaming by what sounded like a gentle stampede. He cocked his ears to the direction of the noise and eyes too. The noise died out but by now Billy could see what looked like a herd of lazy buffalo-like animals. They were all staring in his direction. They did not seem fierce but Billy was not going to take any chance. He started mumbling to himself. 'Billy now is the time to lie calm. Try as much as you can to avoid any confrontation. Co-existence is the principle.' He lay still while from across the pool the other animals stared on at him.

He remembered the order of protocol followed by the Ituri animals. The various animal species took turns to watering. Even then, while the majority drank, a few remained on the lookout against predators. He kept his focus on the animals wondering when the next team would come and if ever the elephants' would appear. As he waited, the cows across the pool also did.

Skuna is a plateau country with savannah type vegetation. Its beauty and productivity formed topics of discussion far and wide. Musicians sung of her. Poets wrote about her. Honeymooners and young romantics all flocked there to enjoy the quiet and beauty. Indeed it was a wonder; a country full of greenery surrounded by desert sands. Her history too was very much attractive and interesting.

Legend had it that hundreds of years ago, it had formed part of a large tropical desert. Close by a river which the natives called the River of Life flowed through it. Initially people lived on the fertile banks. Then at one point a group of people dedicated to serving God in isolation moved into this seemingly remote territory. It suited their lifestyle of self-abnegation as it seemed to portray the scriptural preparedness for the coming saviour.

Although fasting was part of their religious obligation, they also believed that it was wrong in the eyes of the creator to use it as a means to take one's life when other means of survival could be found. So it was that confronted with the need for food in this barren territory that they prayed for a solution. Months and years later nothing seemed to dawn. According to legend one morning they woke up to find a parcel addressed to Kuna the community leader. The entire community gathered to see what it was. Lo and behold, it was a blueprint detailing how the desert could be made productive through irrigation. No one knew the origin of the blueprint but they trusted that it was God's answer to their prayer.

Slowly, carefully and with determination they set out digging irrigation trenches stretching hundreds of miles to the River of Life in accordance with the divinely provided blueprint. They even had to adapt their way of life to fit the project. It became a rule of life to work and pray. Several years later, even before the project was complete, seeds that had lain fallow for millions of years sprouted forming, first strips of greenery then forests with large patches of arable land. Somehow, the massive productivity of the land became more of a test of their own faith. At one point they had wanted nothing of the world and withdrew from it but now instead, they had more than they had ever dreamt of. Food and wine, they had in galore.

The changes in lifestyle tested their commitment to chastity as well. It is believed that one day under the influence of wine, Kuna the community head broke his vow of chastity with one of the female hermits and continued to lead a clandestine life with her. Their secret came into the open when she was found to be with child. The other hermits were disappointed and decided to march to find another dwelling place somewhere else advocating a more stringent return to the original community law of self abnegation and chastity. They left Kuna and Adeta to live as husband and wife. As for the place they called it Skuna which in their dialect meant Kuna's sin.

Kuna and Adeta meanwhile interpreted their fall from grace as a blessing in disguise, for now, though in another way, they lived according to the divine decree: "Be fruitful and multiply".

Kuna's descendants continued the project of transforming the desert in accordance with the blueprint, extending it beyond the stipulations of the blueprint. Rather than confining their work to farming and forest tending they extended their trade to other nations and introduced animal husbandry. As interested parties entered to reap productivity of the land, big cities started to mushroom. Skuna itself became a popular tourist nation, referred to as an Island in the Desert.

One of the most prosperous farms in Skuna stretched as far as the River of Life. It belonged to the Baker family. Mr Baker himself was a very hard working man who dedicated most of his time to his farm. To protect his farm from winds carried by desert storms Mr Baker had created one hundred metre thick belt of forest which he irrigated with water pumped from an underground reservoir.

Billy the Elephant on his way to the unknown entered Skuna through Baker's forest project which led to the stretch of greenery following the River of Life. As Billy lay hidden across the pool waiting for possible sighting of other elephants, the cows on the opposite side stood staring at him. It was like they were playing the "Who Goes First" game.

Back in the farm house, it was a bad day for Mr Baker whose farm workers were on strike because of pay and working conditions. All day he had struggled single-handedly with the job which was normally done by ten men. When the cows went down to the drinking pool, he hurriedly replenished the feeding troughs with hay and silage. With the animals away, he had a few minutes to himself and for a snack. Unfortunately the animals did not return. He decided to peep to see what was happening. Indeed from a distance they were staring at something. He ran back to the office to grab his gun before heading down to see what was happening. As he drew nearer some of the cows lowed at him, and then turned to look across the stream. With his gun on the ready he walked closer and closer to the direction that the animals were staring. There, across the pool he saw something like a rock. 'Goodness me! What do we have here?' he exclaimed. 'A rock? Since when? I have been here all my life and known no rock and just overnight you have one. Strange! Well, I might as well go and take a look. It is possible it has always been there, after all I rarely come this far.'

He walked on but stopped after only a few steps and continued to reason aloud. 'But if that were true, how come these cows are afraid of getting closer? I guess it calls for courage. Nothing to be afraid of, I have the gun. I will see what this is all about...'

From his position, Billy could see the two-legged creature approaching. He had never seen a man before but from hearsay he had built a picture of him. But all this was about to change as he was now coming face to face with a little creature that had made him vagabond. There was nothing spectacular about him. There was something strange which he could not remember if his mother had told him about – the stick he carried with him. Was that the smoke stick with which they had killed the Ituri elephants? he wondered. Was he going to use it on him? Ideas rumbled across his mind but he settled on one. 'I will have to surprise the little creature so that he doesn't use his stick on me', Billy told himself. 'I will have to pretend to be dead'. Despite his size, the very fact a stranger was approaching scared him to the very marrow. He nonetheless did as he had promised. He watched the two legged creature cautiously approach with hands to his gun. Billy did not move and for several minutes Mr Baker stood there watching and wondering how safe it was to touch it. He stretched out his hand and just then Billy rose to his feet. Mr Baker fell to the ground. As for the cows they made off with their tails to the sky.

Billy mumbled a few syllables trying to communicate the few words in man language that Madji the Camel had taught him. 'I mean no harm on anyone. My name is Billy the Elephant. I have travelled a long way looking for home to stay. I will ask the owner for permission.'

Mr Baker rose to his feet. He had to believe what he heard because, the huge beast had all the opportunity to squash him to bits yet he did not. 'I am the owner of this place.'

'Very well Sir', Billy began. Madji has taught him the term sir because men liked it when addressed with. With his limited language he repeated his statement. 'Billy needs a home. Billy has been hiding from baby and walking here two months. Billy needs home. Billy have no home and nowhere to go.' With sorry eyes and dangling trunk Billy made his intentions known.

In the few moments that followed, Mr Baker had a mental review of his own history. He recalled how as a child he had always worked seven days a week running chores for his family. He had never gone to school but thanks to his mother he had mastered his letters at age six and later with a tutor who appeared once a week he was able to read and write. Apart from that all he knew was how to work hard.

One of the most difficult things he failed ever to understand was the church and their doctrine of love. 'Love your neighbour as yourself. Give generously to the needy': had been the weekly sermon of the local pastor. He resented the very idea of giving unless one worked for it. In fact as a matter of principle, he never gave out anything for free. And when it came to remuneration of his employees, he always made sure they got the least possible.

Billy's presence startled him. Somehow something within encouraged him to show compassion. The problem however was that Billy was different, let alone too big to hide. And even if he managed to do such a thing, he could not conceive of any possible way he could be productive. He started to question more. 'Well Mr Elephant, here we do things differently.' He started to rumble on without hiding his disdain for the beast to whom he was talking. 'We are a civilised nation and we have laws. I am sure we can accept you only if you are of some use to our great nation.'

Billy grunted to draw attention. 'Billy speaks elephant. Billy no understanding non-elephant talk. Billy can work for Sir.'

'Why would I want an elephant? I have heard of how dangerous they are to vegetation. They destroy it but have no sense to replace it.'

'Billy will learn if you sir will teach him. Billy will do what you say and will not touch trees.'

'Well that may be true but that is not everything.'

Billy cut in once again. 'Bill needs help. When Billy walked for two months, Billy promised to be good. Billy will do what you say to get home here. No condition is too big.'

'I am sure you can say and promise a lot of good things but if you were in my shoes, would you take for granted words of some uncouth stranger who ignores signs and makes illegal entry?' He kissed his teeth and uttered a mouthful of swear words. Thankfully, Billy did not understand a single one of them. And even if he did desperation would probably have forced him to remain as docile as he was. Mr Baker went on. 'You jolly well knew that this was private land. Of all places you choose to camp close to the pool and scared aware my cows. After all that would you expect me to believe anything you say?'

'Billy is sorry, sir. Billy only speaks and reads elephant language.'

Mr Baker turned towards Billy. 'Tell me one reason why we should let ignorant creatures like you stay here? Of what value are you to Skuna? We don't need economic liabilities.'

Billy went on to argue his case. 'I may look ignorant and indeed I am if reading is the norm, but believe me I am also productive in my own way.'

Mr Baker chuckled a little. 'Well Billy, what can you do?'

'I can provide cheap labour in matters of felling trees and Billy make paths in the forest. All I have to do is walk through the place a few times and behold a road.'

'I guess that just about sums up the case. There is no place for you here. Better turn right round and go back where you came from.'

'I can do a lot more than that', yapped Billy. 'I can provide you with manure. I am talking of top quality and in high quantities, at no charge. Believe me as long as I am well fed, the goods will be delivered wherever you want it. I guarantee there is no need for an intermediary.'

The statement was funny enough to make Mr Baker laugh. Somehow he was beginning to mellow down. At the back of his mind he was already thinking of how best to monetise Billy's presence. 'I guess we can keep you pending official inquiry. You will be kept in isolation until your medical condition is assessed and deemed infection free. In the meantime your presence will be made known to the authorities.'

'I thank you sir', said Billy.

'Well, but do not get any ideas. Right now you will have to move far from this part of the pond. This is for my cows not for you.'

Despite the quarantine and other impositions lumbered upon him Billy was happy to find dreamland. How he was going to be treated and for how long, was immaterial. Right now he was glad to be locked away in a barn which his host provided with assurance of food and water. It would take several days for Billy to get used to life in the poorly lit barn. He learnt to keep away from the unpleasant electric shocks which he received each time he tried to walk closer to the walls.

'Mum I have made it to Glory land. I am not sure of what to expect. Suddenly he cocked his ears for he thought he heard someone familiar talk to him' A kind voice from the inside retorted: "Congratulation indeed it is, but the struggle continues. In life good things tend to come after lots of hardship. You know the saying: "Tender and delicious leaves grow on high trees. If you want them you must work for them." Billy smiled.

The prosperity of Baker's farm depended very much on the lady of the house. Her genius in the money business helped them a great deal. Never at any moment did Mrs Baker yield to the temptation on investing on any business without first making projected analysis of its potential. Besides the farm, they also invested in the stock market and understandably so. Skuna's natural wealth was very delicate. The great majority of its income depended on the money market.

Mrs Baker's routine was predictable. She managed the day to day running of the farm and spent the rest of the day behind her computer watching the stock market. Then in the evening she would get back to balancing the daily transactions. She had just finished her daily duties when her husband came in with that rare and contagious smile of his. He did not wait for her to ask as she always did. 'Honey, guess what kind of surprise I have for you.'

'Well, I have no idea', she replied. Without words she was urging him to let the cat out of the bag.

'We have just added another being to our farm', he said with excitement.

Mrs Baker's smile dwindled. She was expecting a personal gift. 'Oh, I didn't know one of our cows was due so soon.'

'No honey. It is not our animals. This one is different, a stranger that we can use.'

'If that is the case, why don't you tell me about it? I have no time to waste guessing.'

Her tone was resolute. He knew what it meant and he acted at once. 'This afternoon a visitor arrived on our farm by rather unconventional means. He got in through the forest. I have talked to him and he seems pretty harmless. All he wants is a place to stay.'

'I am listening', she urged him on. 'What kind of visitor is he and where does he come from?'

'Oh yes, he is not human kind of visitor' Mr Baker explained with a rather nervous voice.

'I am listening', she reiterated.

'Okay, it is just some stupid elephant. He must have wandered his way into our farm. Personally I don't see any harm in him staying. He is quite a character. You ought to see and hear him talk. All he wants is a place to stay and food in return for his services.'

'I am speechless.'

'You will be even more when you see him.'

'Hubby, look here! I am speechless because your rush judgment is but the beginning of our down fall. Did you know that one elephant eats five times the amount two cows do? Are you prepared to meet all those expenses for a mere useless beast that has nothing to contribute to the farm?' She was out to say her mind. 'Sometimes I wonder if you have any brains in that skull of yours…'

Mr Baker was ready to rebuttal with a tint of sarcasm. 'You are probably right. I have no brains. If I remember well, I swapped them for stones that were used to build our mansion. I am sorry dear wife', he said as he rose to go. Once in the kitchen he helped himself to a glass of water which he really didn't need. Then he headed back with a full battle in his mind. 'I think the problem in this house is that you have been the man for too long. You are one of those masters who have no feelings whatsoever. You do not think of life or others unless it is in monetary terms or productivity.'

Mrs Baker broke in with a rather mocking kind of laughter. 'We must have been blessed with the Holy Ghost for how else could my pagan stingy husband talk of compassion.'

'You may say whatever you want, but the point is that today I also want to be seen as a man in my own house. I have made up my mind Billy is staying right here.'

'Yes sir. I will see to it that he is well provided for. And I am sorry for doubting your sense of judgement.'

Something in the way she responded made Mr Baker embarrassed. He straight away embarked on damage limitation. 'I am sorry honey. I should have called you. I thought we could be compassionate. Of course it does not mean that we have to keep him. Not if his presence is going to jeopardise our lives.'

She smiled at him. 'I am sorry', she began. 'I did not really mean all that I said. Come to think about it we can still have him here as our guest and on our terms. I reckon we can make the best of his presence before he realises that he too has some rights'

'Am I right to think …'

She cut in. 'He will be staying but you and me have to find the best possible way he can benefit us before some righteous person elsewhere intervenes.'

'He says he can manure our land in exchange for food. I say if he is really good at that what stops us from selling some of that manure?'

'I am sure we can find some other uses as well. In my opinion he seems the kind of guy who will cost less but produces more.' She walked to the kitchen to turn on the kettle. 'I think I know just the thing we can get him doing. Just imagine how delighted many of Skuna residents will be to see an elephant for the first time! Most people including me have never seen an elephant at close range. I suggest we create a special cage where he can be displayed to the public. People will pay to see him. It would also be an opportunity to sell some of dairy products, drinks and snacks.' She ran back to rescue the steaming kettle from the stove and to fix tea.'

'Great idea, Mrs Baker. Your genius truly amazes me and I am ever so proud of you. I am the luckiest guy in the world to have someone like you for a wife. I love you', he said as he kissed her on the cheek.

Billy was asleep when the Bakers arrived at the barn where he had made his home. He raised his trunk to acknowledge their presence. 'Billy this is my wife. She is very good and will see to it that you are well fed.'

'Billy is glad to meet the madam of the house. I am sure sir has told madam all about me, in which case there is no need for Billy to repeat the story.'

'Yes indeed. I have heard all about you. I came just to make sure that you are comfortable.'

'Billy is grateful and promises to do whatever the Madam says.'

# Chapter 6

The Baker Tourist attraction business got the attention of locals and foreign visitors. For a fee they queued to see Billy the Elephant. Some came with fruits so as to watch how he used his trunk to manoeuvre them to his mouth. Children came and played with him.

As the business picked up, it became inevitable that Billy would work long hours. Sometimes he was kept in the cage till late at night. The Bakers for their part busied themselves with the proceeds of the business. None really cared about Billy outside business terms. There were times when, apart from the fruits visitor brought, he was left without food. Billy learnt to live on whatever little he had. His weight started to decline but he never let it be a problem.

The strange season that Madji the Camel had spoken about, came. The whole area turned white and was very cold. Billy found it increasingly difficult to cope with the cold. All the same he tried his best to please his hosts. But the problems increased. Long hours without food began to show their effects on the body. Billy started to lose weight drastically and most of the time he felt drowsy. Nonetheless he tried to keep others happy and making jokes about his fatigued body. 'Billy is an elephant and we sleep on our feet.' Of course no word would compensate for his weakening and bony body.

The Bakers in accordance with advice from their veterinarian had no immediate plans for the skinny Billy except to put him under quarantine lest his sickness spread to the rest of the animals. Billy endured his hardships – being caged, quarantined and malnourished. He longed for attention but received none. Nostalgia crept in. Thoughts of his friend Madji the Camel and his mother filled his mind. He started to wonder whether Madji was treated like he was but quickly dismissed the idea. He dismissed the thoughts and concentrated on how he would survive. Each day with its long hours of work was hurting Billy more. His joints ached and his belly grumbled because of starvation.

Billy would have loved to find refuge in the local medicinal herbs, but Skuna was not like Ituri. There were no such shrubs anywhere. He had overheard the Bakers talking that he needed a vet but they would not call one as Billy did not have medical insurance.

Billy's salvation came when a group of activists who fought for animal rights stepped in threatening the Bakers with prosecution. The Bakers gave no fight. And so it was that Billy was put on a transporter and taken to the animal sanctuary to recover from starvation. It was a welcome respite. In no time Billy was back on his feet again.

During his stay at the sanctuary the Bakers never once bothered to visit. Their absence helped Billy decide what he wanted now that he knew he too had rights. His request was to be relocated to any farm apart from Baker's.

Billy's new home was with Samson a circus master who kept among other animals; tigers, lions, leopards and apes. Samson was glad to add an elephant to his collection. He introduced him to his school. Using food and drink he would make animals perform complex routines. Billy liked the treatment and promised himself to master his routines. He made real effort but he was not as agile and fast as the others. Soon Samson's patience started to wear out. He decided to put Billy on diet hoping that might improve his agility.' He informed Billy of his decision.

Billy just smiled as he gave his opinion. 'With all due respect, food rationing does not help Billy. He needs time. Billy has the will and desire to learn. He is merely slow made so by the need to learn to adapt to a different culture and language.'

'I think I have listened to those excuses long enough. I have a business to run and you are becoming a liability. I am a true subscriber to the adage that: *"Who does not work does not eat"*. I might just start applying it on you.'

Billy persisted. 'Very well Sir, you remember teaching me about my rights?'

Samson stared on wondering what Billy was on about. He could recall clearly explaining the rights issue although that was when he desperately wanted to acquire the elephant and win its favour. Yes, he had some rights but what about his rights to get him to do what they had agreed?

Billy did not wait for an answer. 'I insist on my right to a full daily ration of food. Look at the trials I go through, the efforts I put in! So far as I know, my recompense is the food. That is my basic right and I shall demand it.'

'Go right ahead. Don't forget rights do not provide the food you want. I do and it costs me money. As a business person what do I get in return? On the other hand I could let you go roaming about the streets until you meet your death.'

'Maybe that is better than toiling for the master who does not appreciate the efforts you input.'

'I think you have overstepped your boundaries. Don't push me into taking your tusks'

'Billy is sorry to hurt the master's feelings.'

'I suggest you go before I change my mind.' As Billy took his leave, Samson continued talking to himself. He made up his mind to get rid of Billy to highest bidder.

# Chapter 7

Life in the Ituri Elephant kingdom continued to degenerate. What was once thought to be the best means to protect their rights had turned out to be a clear and well calculated way to extinction. No elephant saw the dream freedom. Man who at one time was thought to be the only enemy continued his onslaught of the forest. Through his technical apparatus many elephants got killed. More so the few old bulls whose agility and swiftness had long vanished. One by one they fell under gunfire.

Poachers and loggers dealt hard on the forest. Now it was extremely risky for the elephants. Ironically, whereas some men killed and hunted elephants, other concerned about their welfare hunted and carried them alive to protect their species.

Meanwhile Kobe who had all of a sudden been named King and Ruler for life continued praising his regime. He kept others deceived that the situation in the forest was under control and that no animal especially the elephants had fallen ever since the enacting the Constitution of Survivors. It was clearly a lie contradicted by the daily events and the diminishing number of elephants. He nevertheless remained stuck to his principles. Any elephant who questioned vanished never to be seen, under the secret scrupulous administration of the Special Squad.

The situation was especially pathetic for cows. They were the ones on whom the future of the kingdom rested and yet now the situation was such that the few non-castrated bulls had either fallen under the fire of poachers or, were simply too old to mate. As a result many cows lingered through their heat period without anyone to service them. In the meantime the numbers continued to decline.

Not all cows understood their predicament as resulting from Kobe's policies and method of government. They sought occult interpretation to their predicament. To them the current situation was attributed to ancestor spirits seeking to placate the murder of Ngina. They refused to be silenced and did their business openly. One day they mobilised themselves and stormed into Kobe's palace demanding an immediate audience. Not even the Special Squad could stop them. He was forced to give in to their demands. And so it was that once again the elephants were called to the meeting place.

Kobe, now extremely feeble took to the erected podium. 'Nationals of Ituri', he started, 'feel free to express your minds. I am here at your service and ready to listen and answer any questions.'

The elephants looked at each without word afraid of uttering something that could lead to their death. Fear had long colonised their bones and flowed through their veins. Kobe was about to declare the meeting closed when Nalita took to the stand and spoke; 'I speak on behalf of all girl elephants and indeed for the benefit of all elephant. Years ago in the same place we met to draw a constitution which was supposed to guarantee a safe haven for each of us. Much to our surprise nothing like that has really happened. We continue to be killed by humans; our waterholes are polluted with human industrial refuse and our forest is slowly disappearing. 'She looked across the herd of beasts. They were listening alright. We are not only being killed by humans, King Kobe and his squad have killed many too.'

'Preposterous!' protested Kobe but by now the majority of the elephants were cheering. No one could tell whether they cheered for Kobe or Nalita.

Nalita raised her trunk to restore order. Then she continued. 'Let us be realistic and face the situation. Our dear King Kobe here was the one who hatched up the idea of castrating young bulls. He seemed to forget that none of the few bulls who were not mutilated would live forever. Today we have none, and if at all we have them, they are completely useless. Forgive me for pointing out that you have been a failure in the line of procreation. Then again if you were able to service all of us, our sibling would be weak because of inbreeding. It is in line with that, I on behalf of all the female elephants advocate action to remedy the situation.'

Kobe did not answer the pleas put forth. On the contrary he tried to play them down. 'Well folks, in matters such as the ones raised I have no immediate answers. I shall need time to meet with Special Squad to work out the solution.'

'Sorry King Kobe, your regime has become a liability and it is best if you step down.'

'Why would I do that? You and indeed everyone here know that I am a duly elected leader.'

'I am sure you want to say, a self elected leader.' There was uproar as other elephants showed their agreement. In a voice similar to that made at the inauguration of the constitution of survivors, they raised their discontent.

Members of Special Squad guarding the perimeters, one by one went on the run. They did not want to take any chances because the herd was now entering the riot mode. The others stayed waiting for an opportunity to get at Kobe for having deprived them of the natural right to procreate.

The situation created by the female uprising disturbed Kobe a great deal. He knew he had to act. To act violently would not help as that would imply a complete wipe out of the cows. Again he thought of the members of the Special Squad whose virility he had taken away for his own personal gains. He needed them then but now at his age he couldn't care less. The ground thumping and trunk blowing sent a deafening message. His days were ticking off rapidly. He turned to where Sita was just in time to see his mate make off for the nearest trees. His face dropped in sympathy for his once loyal friend who had sacrificed everything for the great cause. He decided to give it one more shot. He begged Nalita to calm down the furious beasts. In return he promised to consult his leadership team and to arrive at a solution with a few hours.

Nalita persuaded her team but instead of going away they chose to wait without causing any trouble.

Reluctantly, Kobe and a few from his team started their meeting though in low tones. Sita resumed his position. As usual he let Kobe go ahead.

'As you can see what is happening there is very little I can say. Our days as leaders are very numbered. I am tired of denying the truth. I have lied long enough and caused you to do the same. We had better come up with something before they tear us to pieces.'

'Director, I agree. It is time to admit that we have failed. For well over a decade we have ruled this community with an iron hand and deprived them of the truth. Once upon a time we thought castration was the only way of keeping this kingdom at peace. We were wrong and we were endangering our own. The few bulls we relied upon have met their demise and the few still alive are useless when it comes meeting the needs we have today.'

'What must we do?' Kobe asked.

'Well it is not too late to recover', Sita asserted. 'Much as I know, despite our rigid rules and regulations, many bull elephants managed to escape from this forest. They may be living elsewhere. It is to them that we owe the survival of our species. If we treat them well, if we plead with them they may be considerate and return to our rescue. I therefore suggest that we promise them amnesty…'

'Couldn't we do more than that?' another squad member inquired.

'What do you have in mind?' asked Sita.

'Open our border to allow those who want to come back or leave to do so freely.'

The answer was overheard by none squad members who almost immediately applauded it. 'Freedom in and out that is the answer' they trumpeted.

'So be it' declared Kobe, 'amnesty to all exiles it shall be, and we shall open borders to all to come and go as they wish.'

Nalita's crew grumbled. 'We want a total change. Scrap the killer constitution and appoint an interim government. Kobe and his henchmen are free to go.'

Nalita herself stood up. 'I concur. Kobe's time is done. Just step down.'

This time Kobe himself stood to speak. 'If that is the will of the majority, then I Kobe and my team resign with immediate effect. We will however help the transition government until they can govern on their own.'

So it was that Kobe finally let go power. Nalita and her team took over to reshape their habitat. The revolution took place at the time when the entire world rose against the devastations of elephant habitats.

As word about the Ituri amnesty spread to all exiled elephants, some responded by returning. Many however decided against it for having spent several years away, they had kind of become alien to their own culture. Slowly but surely and with international help the Ituri Elephant Kingdom embarked on a major rejuvenation program to clean the rivers, reforestation and to get rid of poachers.

# Chapter 8

Meanwhile in Skuna Billy had been put up for sale to the highest bidder. As it happened, the Skuna National Institute for the preservation of wild life heard of it. Soon Billy was once again on the animal transporter. This time he refused to think about the destination for having been through what he had, he just wanted a new home. He did not have worry because, for his own safety he had been tranquilised. Little did he know that he was finally on his way to the real glory land where he would find companion awaiting.

Meanwhile in her territory Lucy the African elephant watched the wagon, the same type she had ridden in before. It came to a stop near her territory. Unmistakably the smell alerted her that another elephant, a male, was on his way in. Her heart beat faster in excitement. She just couldn't wait to meet someone of her kind. She watched the elephant come out of the wagon and grunted happily. Billy was still dazed up and was happy to lie anywhere.

Later in the day, Billy finally woke up to his senses. Boy was he so glad to have a companion. They spent the day sharing each other's stories. As it turned out to be both of them were from the Ituri. Unlike Billy who trekked his way to Skuna, Lucy had been captured and transported to Skuna. She confirmed that Billy's mother was indeed murdered several days after he had departed Ituri. Billy wept and she wept along with him.

Lucy introduced a different topic for she wanted him to be happy. 'Let us forget the past', she started. 'Look to the future. What has happened has happened. We cannot change it. But we can control our destiny.'

Billy beamed with a smile and agreed. 'Yes indeed, the past is gone. That we have each other is good news. We may not have a forest like our ancestors had, but life goes on. Yes, life is what we make of the time we have.'

Billy and Lucy started their family. Two years later another female was added to their family. In their own way they lived to preserve the species.

# All-of-you the Tortoise

# The Drought

The red soil and clouds of dust said it all. It was drought and there was no doubt about it. The grass was long gone. What was left of trees were dry stems and branches but even that was constantly attacked by the ferocious ant colonies, which seemed to enjoy every minute of these hard times.

That was not all. Famine struck the land. Creatures large and small died of starvation. Those that were able slithered their way to seek life elsewhere. Even then, it was still difficult to survive. En-route, the small and the weak fell prey to the big, strong and the daring opportunists.

In spite of things being hard some creatures stood to benefit from the situation. Among them were scavenging birds. They did not have to go anywhere. Neither did they have to hunt for food. There were always plenty of carcasses to feast on. Fully satiated they would fly to the distant rivers for a drink and return to the feast.

As time went by, it became clear that survival rested not simply on food but also on the ability to endure hard times and to some extent on fitness. The high flyers abandoned the place.

Now the tortoise was the oldest animal in the area. He had lived and seen several such situations come and go. But this drought had nothing to compare with. It had dried up all the ponds and made the ground extremely hard. Usually Mr Tortoise would simply have burrowed his way through the sands and hidden underneath its cool. But to do so in this drought meant roasting his hard shell let alone baking himself to death as many had done. For months he depended on a little crevice under a tree. There he would confine himself moving only whenever it was absolutely necessary. The name of the game was to use as little energy as possible. Yet if he had to survive he had to do something. Somehow he would have to leave the apparent comfort of the crevice and look for life elsewhere. He decided he would make several expeditions out but nonetheless close by. Every night for several weeks he would crawl out of safety hoping to come across some life somewhere else.

It was near sunset. The surviving birds meanwhile assembled under the only thriving cactus tree to decide the next strategy. Everyone was given chance to air their views but the solution was not yet found. Kite the High Flyer started to talk about the land far away where there was plenty of food. 'I have been there. Oh that land! There is nothing to compare it with. The inhabitants too are very kind and hospitable.' He spread out his wings to allow some breeze. 'Ask yourselves. The times when I am not here where do you think I disappear to? He did not wait for any offers but answered his own question. 'You all know me, where else but to that land of abundance and fullness of life! Needless to say, that is why I am as healthy as I look.'

As the birds listened with interest Wagtail jumped in. He was renowned for his meaningless winding speeches. 'If I may cut you short Kite the High Flyer', he began. 'Of course my good friends will appreciate that food is life and I am happy to say that is precisely why we are here. The question which comes to mind is that, if there is plenty there what then are you doing here?'

'Well, there is such a thing as home sweet home. I was born here. I love it here and no matter what I will die here. There may be troubles as indeed there are now, but that does not stop home from being home. Yet on the more mundane side, I do not want to abuse the hospitality of my hosts.' Kite the High Flyer argued.

'Look here folks, let's get to the point. What are we to do to survive this drought?' asked Burrows the Woodpecker. 'Life is getting harder by the day. There is plenty of wood to burrow and yet there is no food. Even if there was any, the drought is making it dangerous for me. Only yesterday, I caused fire by burrowing in the heat of the day. The old stump started smoking and the next minute all I could see was fire. That scared me so much that I am afraid to peck at any tree.' He closed his eyes and gestured as though to peck at the tree he was on. 'Hear me folks, what kind of woodpecker am I if I am no longer burrowing? I cannot afford to lose my *woodpeckerness*. So whether High Flyer is right or not, my word of advice is that we all go after that land of plenty.'

'I am ready to go', said Humming Bird. 'I believe my partner and I have responsibility to ensure the survival of the humming bird species.' His mind wandered. 'When I am dead and have gone to the next world where all the departed creatures go, I want to be able to look down on earth and proudly say, look at the humming birds that descended from me.'

Soon every bird was chanting, 'let us migrate there where there is plenty of food.'

'Surely we are not going to abandon this land of ours', cooed the dove.

Suddenly there was silence. Every bird's eyes looked up. There was a bird flying above. It came and landed on the same cactus tree in which they were. It was a Pigeon the Messenger Bird. He gently worked its way to where the rest of the birds are. 'Good news! Friends, good news!' he cooed hopping from one place to another while the others anxiously waited. 'There is a land of plenty just a day's flight away. I have been there and seen it for myself. The food is plenty. And what is more, the birds there want all of us to go and visit them. Their king is holding a big banquet and he wants us to be there.'

Kite the High Flyer came on again. 'Well that about settles it. Now you all know that I was telling the truth. We shall go as visitors. When the banquet is over we will return here.'

Little Blue the Robin suddenly burst into song. It was so sweet that all the other birds simply sat to listen. For a moment they forgot about their sorrows. He stopped and addressed the others. 'I have an idea. When we get there let us try as much as we can to make friends. I mean we ought to create reasons for wanting to go back in the future.'

From his hiding place Creepy the Tortoise had heard the sweet melody of Little Blue the Robin and had decided to head to the same cactus tree. He started to speak to himself. 'I have never heard such sweet bird songs for ages. There must be something happening there. Who knows, maybe they have found a secret treasure. As far as I know Creepy the Tortoise never misses any opportunity. I will sneak in without warning.'

Of course, he was wrong. There was no way he was going to get there unnoticed. His bad breath always went ahead of him. As he approached the cactus tree every bird had its eyes in his direction. The tortoise started to talk. 'No need for alarm. It is only me. I was just passing by when I heard a sweet melody. I bet it was from Blue the Robin. Oh, how good it felt! I just could not resist it.' He sat at the centre of the gathering. 'Look at these beautiful birds! Praise the creator for them all. All along I thought I was the only survivor here in this seemingly desolate land. I was obviously wrong. Where were you guys hiding? Look at some of you glowing with life!'

There was tense silence as the tortoise went on talking. This was not because they enjoyed what he said. If anything they were disgusted with his presence. But the tortoise never gave up. He went on talking. 'This meeting reminds me of ages ago when we had a long drought. It was similar, but not as bad as this one. All the animals, birds included, met to decide what to do.'

'What happened?' asked Crazy the Cuckoo.

'We decided to temporarily abandon home and sought refuge elsewhere. I do not remember the name of the place we went to but it was certainly rich with food. You could eat as much as you wanted.' Creepy the Tortoise knew that he had to inject in something about travel now. He rolled his eyes and went on. 'As I was saying we had to abandon home for some time. Those creatures like me whom nature has graced with next to zero speed on land, hitched rides on the backs of others. I hitched me a ride on a buffalo back. It was terribly uncomfortable but it was the only way to safety. Any way we stayed there until the rains returned.' He tucked his legs into his shell leaving his head out. 'I am beginning to think that this particular gathering is about the survival of species.' He had overheard the discussion but was merely pretending. 'So where do you intend to go?'

'A long way from here where only flying creatures can reach. We intend to fly at night so as to spend the day time getting used to the inhabitants of the area', replied Pigeon the Messenger.

'I must say this is my lucky day. I will go with you', the tortoise unable to hide his excitement chuckled.

'If I may ask how does Creepy the Tortoise, intend to get there?' queried the Kite.

'I think that is not the issue at the moment. Just tell me where you are going and I will find my way there', replied the tortoise. 'I told you that a long time ago thanks to the kindness of the buffalo I survived death from drought. I was hoping the same could happen this time round. Of course if no one is willing to help, somehow I will make my way there. If you will, please be kind enough to name the direction, the tortoise will plan accordingly. It may take days but I will surely get my stinking body there. I will make sure I travel at night when it is a little cooler. Several day or even weeks later, I will get there. That is if I will still have some bits of energy left. If I fail, well that is life. At least I would have tried. Best of all, I would probably end up being food to some animal or bird of prey like Kite here. His emotive speech got the birds looking at each other wondering whether it would be fair to leave the tortoise to die in the drought stricken country.

'Very well then' said Kite the High Flyer. 'We intend to go far away to the land where the earth touches the sky. It is not far from where the sun goes to bed. It will take a good deal of flying too. From all looks it is certainly not the kind of land one will crawl to. And even if you did, it would take you several weeks. Who knows? For Creepy the Tortoise this could even be years.' He let open his wing span to let off some heat and then resumed. 'To cut the story short, the place is very far. By the time you crawl your way there, this home of our will probably be teeming with life again.'

The tortoise did not give up yet. He knew time had come to use both his charm as well as tricks. He started to tell stories. 'We tortoises are not in the habit of asking for favours unless the situation was dire. If I may ask, ever heard of any tortoise that asked anybody for help? No. We take care of ourselves. When things go wrong we withdraw into our shells until things change. On the other hand tortoises like helping. History has it that we have been behind the survival of many animal species.' He changed his tone in to a rather cheerful one. 'By the way, how would you birds like to enter history as heroes?'

'What on earth are you driving at? As far as we birds are concerned we have been invited to another kingdom. We will be leaving shortly and we will stay there for a few days and possibly until the rains return', explained the kite.

'I am sure you were planning on taking me along', commented the tortoise.

'Not really. The invitation is for birds not tortoises. Besides tortoises do not fly' exploded Kite.

'I know that and that is why I want you to make history. Fly with the tortoise and your names shall live forever. Don't ask me how because you know the answer. The tortoises leave longer than all creatures.' He made a brief burst of laughter. 'You know I am so old that I do not even know how old I am. For most of you here, if not all, I have known your great grandparents. Anyway, forget the past. I am a tortoise and I am sure I will still be alive fifty years from now.'

'You mean to say, if you do not starve to death.'

'If that be the case, I pray I die peacefully without having to haunt anyone. I am not threatening anyone but it is quite obvious you do not want to be haunted by the tortoise. It is the worst thing that could ever happen to anyone.' He raised his body off the ground. 'Unfortunately for you, there is nobody here to tell you historical facts.'

'What facts?' Heron the Grass Walker asked.

'If you should know, one of you great grand uncles once swallowed a baby tortoise. He had been warned against it but he refused to listen. Anyway, his whole life turned into a mess. He would do anything to inflict pain on himself. He used to scrape the termite hill open then when the angry soldier ants came out to fight the intruder, he would lay there to be bitten by the ants. My friends and I used to drag him out to mud to sooth his bleeding body. The poor heron did a lot of crazy things. Nobody but the tortoises knew that the poor bird was haunted. Any way one day, they found him fighting a tree trunk. He was seriously hitting it hard with all his might, when a fox made a meal out of him.' Tears started to flow down his little eyes. 'I am sorry but I just can't bear it. I do not want the same thing to happen again. I do not want to see anyone crash his bones as that poor heron did. Just imagine if a baby tortoise could cause such, what harm could a giant like me inflict! I leave you to decide.'

It was quite clear that the tortoise was not going to give up. The more they tried to discourage him, the more time they wasted. Somehow, the story of the haunting had driven fear into the birds. They gave in and accepted to take Creepy the Tortoise with them. It was agreed that each bird would give him a few feathers with which to make wings and to cover his body so that he looked like a bird. The weaverbirds offered to knit them together. Wax from deserted beehives would also be used to hold them on to his body. With specially fitted elastic strings attached to his legs, he was able to flap them up and down.

In the days that followed Creepy the Tortoise was given his wings. Kite the High Flyer was the one charged with teaching the tortoise how to fly. After several trials on anthills and on trees, Creepy the Tortoise was deemed ready and like the rest he waited for the day.

# The Flying Tortoise

When the day finally came, the tortoise and the birds gathered to begin their journey. The kite and other bigger birds were to fly side by side with the tortoise. They were about to set off when the tortoise came up with one of his stories. 'Pardon me. I know I am older than most of you here. I have had a good life. I have seen things happen. Things good and bad things, I have seen them all. I have even seen creatures humiliate themselves in front of others. I pray that does not happen with us. But if it does I hope it remains where it happened.'

'Get down to earth tortoise. You are beginning to waste precious moments. What exactly do you want to say?' Kite queried.

The tortoise took on the opportunity. 'When I was little', he began with gusto, 'we were in the habit of taking false names each time we went on a visit. The idea was that, you keep your name pure but spoil the nickname. I am suggesting that we take up false names. I know all eyes will be set upon us. Any slight mistake one makes will be noted. Personally I would prefer to make mistakes but have them pasted on my false name. Whether you like the idea or not, as from now my name is no longer Creepy the Tortoise. My new name is *All-of-You*.'

'What sort of name is that?'

'Never mind, just call me *All-of-You*. I have a reputation to protect and will allow no minor indiscretion taint it.'

The birds too decided to take up false names. Then they set off on their way to visit their friends. They flew all through the night non-stop and arrived their destination shortly after sunrise. They were received well. Even though the tortoise was visibly different nobody asked questions. In the introductions he had been presented as belonging to a rare bat family.

The party began with snacks. The hungry visitors delved into it in silence. There was no such a thing as food being bad or good. At this moment in time, they were happy to be fed. After all, they could not afford such privileges in their land.

The tortoise had had many parties in his life. He knew pretty well that the first helpings were simply the beginning. The best was still to come. So he ate the snacks reservedly. Indeed less than an hour later, a team of waiters and waitresses started to flow in with the food. The guests meanwhile looked on with amazement. Surely, they were going to fill their empty grumbling bellies.

The food was well laid down ready to be eaten. The waiters and waitresses went away in single file. The head of the team bowed down inviting the guests to their meal. 'Enjoy your meal', he said and turned around to go.

Just then Creepy the Tortoise fired one question. 'If you do not mind, who is the food meant for?'

'Oh, it is for all of you', replied the waiter with a smile.

'Thanks and no further questions', said the tortoise. No sooner had the waiter gone than the tortoise turned to his friends. 'You heard it with you own ears. The food is meant for me. He said it.'

'He said it was for all of us.'

'I beg your pardon. He said it was for *All-of-You*. And that my dear friend happens to be my name. Remember we changed names on the way here.'

'Wait a minute! Do you want to say that we are meant to be simply watching you eat?'

'For a time being, I would say yes. I mean you may have to wait until your own share comes. Or is that too much to ask?'

'I guess not, although I cannot fathom how our hosts came to know only your name', argued Burrows the Woodpecker.

'You may recall on arrival that I wasted no time. I told them my name then.'

So it was that the tortoise ate all the food he could. What he could not eat he made sure it was taken away before the rest on his team could help themselves to it. The other guests waited for their share of food but it never came. Later on, in the evening when another meal was served, the tortoise once again claimed it using his false name. The birds were clearly at loss. They had travelled all the way to this land expecting plenty but now it was turning out differently. They grumbled amongst themselves.

At night whilst the tortoise with his belly full slept peacefully, hungry and angry birds held a secret meeting. Some birds wanted to leave the tortoise behind but others at the instigation of Kite the High Flyer persuaded them not to. It was argued that such an act would not only shame them but also spoil their relationship with their friends. However, it became clear that they decided they would take the tortoise back and then return to continue their stay. The journey back was to be made in the day despite the heat.

As the new day came, the birds rose earlier than the tortoise. They sat in the sun with wings outstretched to warm themselves. The tortoise joined them too. When breakfast was served, the tortoise once again appealed to his name antiques and ate all the food.

Creepy the Tortoise was just bracing himself for the activities of the day when Kite the High Flyer announced that they were leaving for their land immediately. Creepy the Tortoise tried to protest but in the end gave in. He had to fly back with the rest. Any way he had nothing to lose. The food he had eaten was enough to keep him going for many weeks ahead. In fact he planned to go on hibernation as soon as they got back to their land.

Kite the High Flyer had had a quiet word with their hosts assuring them that they would be gone for a few hours but they would return. There was no need for goodbyes. They swarmed into the air making sure that Creepy the Tortoise was in their midst just in case he needed some boost at lift off. Of course there was more to it than keeping him in the middle. After the last flight, his wings desperately needed retouching but no bird was in the mood to volunteer to help let alone to warn him about it. They just flew on in silent formation.

The tortoise, excited and feeling good with all the food he had eaten urged the rest to fly even higher. They did so, knowing that such great heights would be their way of exacting their revenge. They knew that the wax that held together the wings they had made for the tortoise would melt any time now. They had been flying for nearly two hours when suddenly the tortoise began to lose height rapidly. Rather than flying towards home, the birds started to descend with him.

Scared of the impact of the inevitable fall the tortoise begged and cried for help. But the birds just descended with him. Creepy the Tortoise screamed out; 'Help me, I am going down!'

Kite the High Flyer swooped down at the same speed as the falling tortoise and shouted out loud, 'I thought Mr All-of-you did not need anybody's help.'

'Of course I do need help. I have always done', cried the tortoise.

'Perhaps you did. This time nobody will help you. No, you think you are crafty? You used us and you insulted our generosity. Now Mr All-of-you, you are on your own.'

'No no. I was wrong I will never do it again. I will repay all of you tenfold.'

'No mate. It is all over. You will soon crash into pieces. Unfortunately the food you ate will be of no use to you. Actually if you had eaten less, I am sure you would be fine. There would be a fair chance of surviving with minor injuries. May be I would even put you on my back. But no, I am going to watch you crash to pieces. Then we will leave you to die.'

'What good would my death serve, cried the tortoise?'

'Nothing really but let's call it revenge sweet revenge. We will enjoy watching you take that Humpty Dumpty crash. And if for some reason you do survive, I promise we kites and indeed every bird of the kite family will hunt your kind for food. We will break and drink your eggs, we will eat your little ones as soon as they hatch and we will forever work to tear out your shell. Call it a war of claws against shells has just been started.' He led the birds back to a suitable height and returned to continue their visitation.

Mr Tortoise's flight was definitely coming to an end. The wings fell off leaving his rounded body propelling like a stone. He tucked his head and legs into his shell and prepared for the worst. Then with aloud thumping sound, he crashed to the ground smashing into a bundle of pieces held together by few gooey tissues. He was still alive but completely immobile. He groaned in agony. Then as though to add salt into injury the kite and other flesh eating birds perched close by. They were laughing at him. 'Creepy, I want you to know that we did not mean any harm. We are simply paying you back. Let's call this your reward for being greedy. We want you to know that even if you don't live to tell the story, we will.'

But the tortoise continued to mourn in agony. 'Oh, I am dying.'

The kite in return answered: 'That much I know. Unfortunately, it is going to be a long time before you die. Call it dying slowly. Then again, it is better than being eaten by me. I am going to repeat what I said earlier to make sure that you never forget it. As from today, that is if you survive to tell the tale, the entire family of kites will be after your offspring for food.'

'But that is not fair.'

'So too was eating all the food at the expense of those who helped you. Anyhow, may you die painfully', Kite the High Flyer said. 'Sorry I almost forgot, the ants will soon be here to suck out all the tissues from you.' Kite and the birds flew away.

# Fixing back the Pieces

Creepy the Tortoise continued to groan in pain. He was lucky he had crashed into fairly cool grassland. The decomposing leaves had actually been instrumental in reducing the impact of the fall. The question now was that, how long would it be before he died?

Shelly the Snail had had a pleasant night in the foliage. She had eaten enough and settled under a bush nearby. She was awakened by the tortoise's groans. 'What on earth is going on?' She popped out her antennae towards the direction of the sound. 'This is strange. I have lived here all my life but never heard anything like this. I mean, in this land we all respect each other. Nobody bothers me when I sleep. But this stranger, where is he from? I suppose I must really go to see what is happening.'

She let herself out of the shell and made straight to the direction. Creepy the Tortoise continued to groan in agony. 'Is there anyone here who can help me? I am dying. I need help.'

Shelly the Snail arrived and wasted no time. 'You there, how dare you come and disturb my rest!'

'Please, I beg you I need some help. I am dying.'

'I am not sure about that. Your voice is too strong for a dying creature.' She drew even closer and looked at the tortoise. He looked like a piece of stone that had cracked to pieces. Fortunately every piece seemed in place. 'Tell me whoever you are, is that how the creator made you? I do not mean to be disrespectful but I cannot help being amazed. You look just like pieces of some shattered shell.'

'I once had a shell. One beautiful and strong shell.'

'Then what happened? What made you that way?'

The tortoise once again groaned. 'Oh, I am dying.'

'Well, mister or whomever you are, how am I expected to know where the pain is? You whole body looks like one good mess. And if you want to know the truth, it stinks as well.'

The tortoise moaned on, 'the whole of my body is in pieces. My shell is broken.'

'I must warn you. This land is not as kind as you may think. Soon, lots of ants and maggots will be teeming on you. You are just the perfect state for them. They all love the juicy bits and once they start you are history.' Shelly crawled round. Then she exclaimed. 'Look at the state of you! Mister you need to get yourself sorted real fast before flies descend on you. Nasty insects they are! They suck your juice and yet at the same time they lay their eggs on you. Hours later your body is reduced to nothing but maggots.'

Creepy the Tortoise was even more scared. 'Please do something before maggots eat me.'

'I am sure we can do something but first things first. What happened to you?' She touched his shell. 'In the name of goodness, your shell is even harder than mine. I am sure it must have taken some kind of sledge hammer to bring it to this state.'

'No, I fell from the sky.'

'Oh goodness me! This is becoming even more interesting. You fell from the sky? How did you get there without wings? Are you some kind of divine creature?'

The tortoise was not in the mood for any questions but at the same time he realised his survival depended on his answers. He decided to tell the truth after all he had nothing to lose. 'The birds helped me', the tortoise began. 'Where I came from there is no food because we have had a long drought. The birds decided they were going far away to look for food. Well, they were kind enough to let me fly with them. They even made wings for me and taught me to fly. But when my wings fell off, they refused to help me.'

'Now that is what I call wickedness. That is malicious.'

Creepy the Tortoise broke in. 'I think I am the one to blame. I was very wicked to them. I tricked them and I ended up being the only one to eat the food that was meant for all of us.'

'You mean to tell me it is just a question of greed. Is there anything else I should know?'

The tortoise had nothing to lose. He told his story. As the tortoise began his story Shelly's mind wondered back to her own experience with the witch. She too had been greedy.

'I will help you. I will patch up your shells but they will never go back to what they used to be. In my opinion it is better to be alive than dead.'

Shelly set out to patch up the tortoise. She pushed the pieces of shell together and then crawling over his body stuck the bits in place. All she had to do was to crawl over his body. 'Greed is a bad thing. Unfortunately we all learn about it when it is all too late. I am not blaming you. I myself have lived such a situation. I have been greedy and paid for it dearly.'

The tortoise became curious but did not want to ask. 'Friend, I swear by my life. I will never walk the road of greed again.'

'I was just about to ask you to make that promise.' Shelly's art work put the tortoise together again. He was accordingly instructed to stay immobile for several days while his body healed. Shelly herself remained in the neighbourhood. Seven days later, the tortoise was able to crawl around without much pain. Shelly was happy with her handwork. She sat down the tortoise for she had something to tell. Then she began to pour out her heart.

'Once upon time I was a beautiful little creature. I was neither a fish nor some land creature. I lived on both land and sea. I spent most of my time eating on land. One day, I found this garden rich with fruits. Each time I took out my hand to pick up one, I saw another one much better than the first. Naturally I would let that go and try to reach for the next. Well, it was the hardest job to choose. I just could not make up my mind. I kept climbing from one branch to another. Any way I finally settled to one fruit. Oh, how sweet and refreshing. I do not know what happened but I am sure I smelt some beautiful cuisine. When I looked down, there was this cauldron right under the tree. From the scent I could swear it was very delicious.'

'What happened?' Creepy the Tortoise curiously enquired.

Shelly signalled to Mr Tortoise not to interrupt. 'I waited for a long time but could not see anyone around. Anyhow I decided to go for it. I discovered that all I had to do was to let go the branch that I held onto and I would be right inside the pot. And that is just what I did.' She closed her eyes to imagine the taste of the food. The tortoise meanwhile remained with the mouth agape.

'As I was saying, I was right inside the pot. How glad I was when it turned out that it was just lukewarm! Well, it was not as solid as I expected. It was some kind of gruel. I was not particularly worried because I knew I could always swim out of it. I tasted a little and it was delicious beyond temptation. Anyway I decided I would finish it before I left the place. That is precisely what I did. Slowly but surely, little by little I ate it. You know I even forgot all about the potential danger that could be involved. I did not think of the fact that whoever left the food there would come back sometime. To the cut the story short, the owner of the food came and found me just about to finish it. Worse yet the owner was some mean witch.'

'Goodness me! A witch!' yapped the tortoise.

Shelly simply nodded her head and antennae in approval. 'A witch was the owner of the porridge.'

'What happened?'

'Well, look at me! The witch put a spell on me. That is why I have a shell on my back. Mind you it is not really bad. Matter of fact it has become a blessing. When I am attacked, I retreat inside it.'

Mr Tortoise felt he could chip in his views. 'That must have been a good witch' he began. 'I mean I am a very old creature but I have never come across a good witch.'

'Wait a minute', Shelly cried out. 'The spell goes further than simply carrying the shell. My diet too is affected. I am condemned to eating rotting vegetation for the rest of my life. Of course from time to time I grab a few blossoms and young leaves. Otherwise, my food is rotting leaves.'

'I am terribly sorry', Mr Tortoise said to Shelly who was now crying.

'Somehow I would get used to my diet but the wicked witch went even further. Wherever I pass I have to leave behind a trail of some slimy substance. She said it would constantly remind me never to steal anybody's porridge again.' Shelly suddenly smiled. 'That slimy jelly is not after all useless.'

'What do you mean?'

'Well I just used it to put you back together. I am beginning to think that nothing is really useless. The same slimy stuff protects me. It keeps away ants.'

'In the olden days we used to call your experience a blessing in disguise.'

'Any way now that you are whole again, I would like you to make a promise never to return to the vice of greed.'

'I promise. I will never be greedy again. I am also going to be like you. I will eat only vegetation all my days.'

'You better stick to your promises otherwise something really nasty could happen to you next time. However, I must remind you that, your wounds will heal but your shell will never go back to its original state. It will always remain patchwork. May it always remind you of this incident? You are welcome to stay anywhere within this land until such a time as you are fit enough to go to your home.'

'Thanks ever so much. I will always remember you.'

'And I will never forget the rewards of greed.'

Shelly the snail crawled away into her hide out. Creepy the Tortoise too found himself a home. Immediately he began to plan how to return to his land.

# Douglas the Dog

# Chapter 1

Once upon a time all animals great and small lived in one big forest. Within that great home of theirs there existed even smaller communities bound together by friendship and mutual respect. They mixed freely sharing parties and ceremonies whenever they could. Each small community constituted several homesteads.

Now Douglas the boy Dog and Tembo the girl Elephant lived in one homestead. They were not husband and wife as such but just good friends bound together by a blood pact. By virtue of her large size, Tembo naturally volunteered to take responsibility over food. She would do all the hunting and other activities connected with it.

Douglas the Dog was in charge of looking after the home and the little ones. It was deemed the best thing for him because of his natural ability to decipher different smells even at a distance. He was particularly going to be useful in cases of tracking enemies.

Tembo had twin calves, the male one called Kasajja and the female one called Kawala. As a precaution Tembo the Elephant had laid down some ground rules to be obeyed by all who lived in her homestead. They were all designed for the safety of the little ones. One of the regulations banned Douglas the Dog from ever eating bones. This was to avoid bone splinters from injuring the little ones. Douglas accepted it because he valued his friendship with Tembo.

Doing without a bone was the greatest sacrifice that Douglas the Dog would ever make. He knew it but all the same promised to abide by the ruling. As a matter of fact from day one his thoughts never left the bones. He dreamt about bones and often times visualised himself eating one. Nights were even more treacherous for him. In his sleep, he would dream that Tembo had lifted the edict banning him from eating bones and that she was actually asking him to eat one. Unfortunately he always woke up to find no such a thing.

In attempt to keep bones away from Douglas the Dog, Tembo made sure that all the bones were extracted from any meat that was brought home. She would put bones in a collection pile a few yards from their home. With time the pile grew higher and higher creating a huge mountain of bones. Tembo never once gave thought about how the mountain of bones affected Douglas. If anything she acted on the conviction that Douglas would never break their agreement. In reality the smell of flesh left over the bones only heightened Douglas' dreams and fanned the urge to crack one.

One day, Tembo who was about to set out on her routine hunting, summoned Douglas for the usual debrief and reminders of his obligations. 'I will be gone for several hours. Take good care of the little ones. Especially keep an eye on Kawala. She is a lot more active than her brother Kasajja and likes wandering away into the forest. Above all remember your own vows.'

'Vows! What vows?' bewildered Douglas asked.

'Remember you promised never to taste a bone', said Tembo with a smile.

'Oh, so that is what they call vows? I didn't know. In any case I think you are beginning to think that I am stupid. Do you think I can go back on my word? And if I would why haven't I done it since?' responded Douglas in a rather high voice.

'I am sorry. I did not mean to offend you', explained Tembo as she began her journey.

Douglas whose mind was truly focused on bones called after her. 'Tembo, I am sorry. I shouldn't have snapped at you.'

'Don't worry about it. It is all forgotten.' She lifted her trunk to reveal the biggest smile ever. It was inviting a response. Douglas smiled back at her. There was a joyous silence as the two friends cherished each other. Tembo would have loved to stay on but she had a job to go to. She set off. 'I am off, mate. Take care of yourself and the calves' said Tembo.

'Say no more', Douglas barked.

Tembo started off but stopped after just two paces. 'Remember keep an eye on Kawala.'

Douglas just wagged his tail. 'May good luck follow you on your mission', said a bemused Douglas. By now his mind was once again focused on bones. He stole a quick look at the pile and then turned back to continue to watch Tembo as she disappeared behind bushes. He ran a few yards in Tembo's direction just to make sure that she was completely gone. He sniffed at the air in search of her scent. Apart from the trail left in her tracks she was not anywhere near. She was truly gone.

Douglas was now alone. A stone's throw away the two elephant calves enjoyed themselves wallowing and rolling in the mud. The temptation to eat the bone seemed to hit even harder driving Douglas to intense speculation. He began to talk to himself. 'Tembo is not here and will not return until late in the afternoon. I am sure if I ate one bone she would never know.'

The more he thought about the bones, the more his mouth watered. He smiled and as he did so, his saliva dripped onto the ground. 'I made a vow to Tembo that is true. In hindsight I think I was being unreasonable. How could I bond myself against something which is supposed to be natural part of my life? He paced about tail between legs and tongue creating a visible trail of his saliva. He stopped again to peep at the little elephants who weren't at all bothered. 'A vow is a vow but I think there is still room to unbind myself. I will wait for Tembo to come back then I will tell her face to face that the pact is over. Unless she decides to draw up new terms, I shall move out and start living like a dog again.' He growled showing his canines. 'That is how I will be. I will be a dog with attitude', he told himself. He decided to walk round the pile of bones and again stopped to talk to himself. 'But what will I be doing until then? May be I should just eat one. After all there is no one around. I think I will eat one, clean my mouth and wait for Tembo.' He made up his mind to eat at least one bone.

So it was that Douglas the Dog yielded into the temptation. He walked straight to the pile and selected two with succulent bits of meaty tendons. He was so careful not to leave any trails. Hidden behind the mountain of bones away from the calves, he lay down and attacked the bone with all ferocity and excitement. In no time he was done with one. He stood up and took a quick look around in case there was someone watching. There was no one and even Tembo's calves seemed completely taken by their play. Well, just a small one before I call it a day', he said as he took another bone. Once again he settled down and started to eat the bone. He closed his eyes in enjoyment as the bone crashed under his teeth. The cracking sound of the bone felt heavenly but it was loud enough to be heard by someone else.

Kawala and Kasajja unaccustomed to the sound of cracking bones ran to see what was happening. They found Douglas the Dog with a huge bone on his front legs, eyes closed and head inclined sideways as the teeth did the work. It was Kawala who spoke first.

'Uncle Douglas, what are you doing?' Kawala asked.

Douglas who had not noticed their arrival tried to cover his shock. He immediately cooked up the story. 'Oh, I was just cleaning my teeth. Not really. I mean I was just playing the game that only dogs do.'

'But why doesn't our mother also do it? Kasajja asked.

Douglas forced himself to laugh before answering. It is because you know the answer. 'It is because your mother is not a dog. She is an elephant.'

'Now I know why she has been collecting all these bones. It is because she is an elephant and elephants do not know what to do with bones' responded Kasajja.

'I couldn't have put it any better than that', barked Douglas.

While Kasajja was impressed with his own discovery, Kawala was up to something else. She demanded to try the game. 'Uncle Douglas can we try one bone game?'

'I don't think that is such a brilliant idea because like your mother, you are elephants not dogs.'

'Uncle Douglas, could we just pretend to be dogs for a minute? We promise not to tell mother.'

'You should never try this dog game in any way because there is a long story behind it. However, if you behave yourselves may be one day I will tell you why dogs play with bones', explained Douglas temporarily letting go his grip over the bone. He resumed his talk before the two baby elephants could ask any further questions. 'Then again I may never have the time. I might as well do it now', he added.

'Hurray!' yelled the little elephants.

'I see you like the idea but there is just one thing I want to request of you. Promise me that you won't tell your mother about this', requested Douglas.

'We promise', said the little elephants in unison.

'Thanks. But there is just one more thing that I should say. Will you allow me to finish with this bone first?'

'Sure, why not?' the little elephants once again replied in unison.

'Of course, I knew you would understand', commented Douglas reassuringly. He once again shifted the bone between his paws as he prepared the big and final bite. He bit the bone with all might sending splinters all over the place. One piece flew in the air and lodging itself on Kasajja the little elephant just above the eye. The little elephant screamed and fell back in agony as blood gushed all over the face. Unfortunately as he fell back, he landed onto a sharp wooden peg which was used to fence in the homestead. It lodged itself right inside through the ribs before breaking off inside. The damage to the internal organs was not immediately apparent but Kasajja was staggering like in a delirium.

Douglas rushed to pull out the bone splinter from near the young bull's eye. Blood gushed out from the broken veins. He barely noticed the fatal wound at the side. 'Kawala grab a few leaves now', commanded Douglas as he placed his paws to apply pressure and sooth where the bone had struck. He licked the blood with his tongue while blowing into it at the same time. He folded the leaves and stuck them on to the wound. 'What you need right now is to lie down while I fix your wounds.' He led Kasajja to his pen and with his hand rubbing gently he sang his favourite lullaby to him. Soon little Kasajja's eyes started to close with his trunk twitching in a very unusual way manner. Both Douglas and Kawala thought he was near sleep. They left him in the pen to sleep. Douglas returned to clear the mess.

Unfortunately for Douglas, Kawala was poised to raise trouble. 'So that is why mother insisted that you don't eat bones. It is dangerous. It can kill and now my brother is going to die', remarked Kawala.

'Do not worry. Your brother is perfectly okay. All he needs is a little sleep and soon you will see him jumping up and about. Next time you see him, he will be as good as new.' He looked at Kawala reassuringly. 'Well, now I will just clear up this place and then we shall start talking business. As a matter of fact, I could use your help. You know the sooner we finish the more time we have to talk business.'

Kawala was impertinent. She argued back. 'What is there to talk about? I will tell my mother all about what happened. This is something she ought to know. It is her baby lying there in pain.'

'My girl, you dare not do such a thing. If you do I will never give you any of my goodies. You know I am capable of it.' He waited to hear Kawala's reply. There was none. He went on with a changed tone. 'Anyway, you better do what I say otherwise I promise to make your life so miserable that you will start wishing that you were never born.'

Kawala laughed. 'I don't think so. I will run away to the forest to find my father. He is big. He is so strong and fierce that even trees give him way.' As she spoke her trunk swung from side to side, up and down. Her eyes shone. 'I have seen him fight and believe me he will squash you with his foot until you are as good as mud', Kawala threatened.

Douglas was no stranger to elephant wrath. As a little pup, he had seen one a giant biddy-eyed elephant destroy with one stump the log that had housed them. Now as Kawala spoke Douglas could just about picture the scene but he was not going to back down without a fight. He knew that it was time to put up a threat to mitigate a threat. 'What makes you think that I will allow you go that far?' he growled. 'Try it and see for yourself how my dog friends will be glad to make a meal out of you. Just imagine your flesh being ripped out bit by bit starting from the soft tissues on the backside. They will burrow through you like a worm eating the insides. By the time your mother comes every bit of you would have been eaten and everywhere licked clean of blood.'

Kawala was scared but she was not going to give up easily. If anything she had her own plans and this was a perfect opportunity to lay them bare. 'Uncle Douglas,' she called. 'May be we could strike a deal. You know the kind of pain my mother can inflict on anyone with her trunk. She can wind it round you and squash your bones. She can even beat you so hard and fast that you will wish you had not messed with her. I do not want that to happen to you.'

Douglas was getting impatient. 'Listen Kawala if you have anything to say do so now. As you can see I have a job to do.'

Kawala went on. 'As I was saying, my part of the deal is that you do exactly what I say. I am talking of being allowed to go to see my friends as and when I feel like. Of course I mean when mother is not home. I want the freedom to roam the forest. Shall I take it that we have a deal?'

Douglas the Dog was glad to hear this. In fact he was prepared to do whatever it took to bury the incident. Just in case Kawala would see it as a weakness in him, he pretended not to like it. He turned to Kawala. 'How do you propose to deal with poachers?' He asked.

'I don't think you should worry about that. The question is do you want a deal or not?'

Douglas did not want to appear to have no options. 'Well, I do not normally give in to blackmail but I suppose I can make an exception. Let it be just this one time.'

Kawala was so excited that she decided to lay further demands right away. 'Listen Uncle Douglas, from now on you have no say over me. At least that will be it as long as mother is out. I suggest you use your discretion before you say anything new.'

Kawala's words were nothing short of threat. She looked serious and meant everything. Douglas the Dog was caught in a fix. He had no choice if he had to keep the peace with his friend Tembo. Reluctantly he accepted Kawala's offer. 'You are asking too much but let's say it is all accepted.'

'I am glad you are being sensible' retorted Kawala.

'I suggest you go to play meanwhile I clear up this place' urged Douglas.

'Actually I intend to go out into the gardens, then to my friends. I might even want to go down the forest', Kawala said ready to exploit the deal she had just won.

Douglas the Dog cut in, 'you may go anywhere but not the forest. I beg you not to do so, because you might meet your mother there. Actually, I would suggest that you stay home today, then tomorrow you can do whatever you like.'

Kawala smiled. 'Uncle Douglas you have just made my day. I will leave you to clear the place.'

# Chapter 2

Douglas the Dog had just cleared up the place when Tembo the Elephant returned from the hunt. He proceeded to welcome her. 'Welcome back. It is a rich harvest that one', commented Douglas.

'As they always say, everything comes with a little of hard work. I worked hard and was able to bring home all this. I am sure it will be enough for days', Tembo proudly answered.

'Oh yes. It is more than enough. I pray it does not go bad', joked Douglas.

Tembo was anxious to have everything out of her hands. She addressed Douglas; 'Since I have done the hunting, may I suggest that you help me feed the young ones?'

'No need to worry. I will do that', said Douglas his mind focused on the injured elephant. He was thinking of how to keep Tembo from discovering what had happened. 'If you do not mind I would like to try out a different method of feeding Kawala and Kasajja. I want them to take turns. Matter of fact I have talked to them about it and they are very willing to try it.'

'Douglas, do not disturb me. I don't really care provided everyone has enough food', retorted Tembo.

'I thought as much myself' Douglas happily said. He rushed to where the two elephant calves were sleeping. 'Well my dear friends. Your mother is back and I can assure you there is quite a lot to eat. I suggest only Kawala will come with me. As for Kasajja I will bring him his share in bed', Douglas explained.

His suggestion was met with joy from Kawala. She knew the trick was working. And yet at the same time she was worried about her brother Kasajja. 'Uncle Douglas', she begun, 'I think the situation is not as good as we may think. Little Kasajja has neither moved nor talked since you brought him in to sleep. Even flies seem to be taking advantage of his eyes. Do you think he is dead? Oh yes, I

93

remember mother used to say never let an injured calf sleep because it easily relapses to unconsciousness and to death. You killed him.'

'Shhhhhh!' Said Douglas his paw in the mouth beckoning for silence. 'I am sure he is merely sleeping'. He moved closer to feel the pulse. There was none. Little Kasajja was dead. Douglas was speechless and began to shiver immediately.

Kawala began to suspect the worst. She demanded to know what was happening. But Douglas the Dog knew his way round such situations. He came up with a new story. 'There is nothing wrong. It is only my jaws. They hurt real bad but they are all right now. Come on! It is your turn to eat. But do not forget our little secret.'

'Your secret is safe with me', Kawala assured Douglas as they walked to eat.

Douglas the Dog lay down to watch Kawala eating. He did not seem concerned about how long Kawala would take eating. He was worried about the death of Little Kasajja. Tembo however, noticed it. Worried that Kawala would eat more than Kasajja, she complained. Her comment sounded more like a reminder. Uncle Douglas you seem to have forgotten Little Kasajja. He ought to be here now.'

'You are quite right. I was just going over my life. Oh yes. I was daydreaming. I suppose it is old age', he said as he got up. He called to Kawala. 'Off we go. It is your brother's turn.'

Kawala joined him and walked without word. When they were well away from Tembo, Douglas addressed Kawala in a whisper like voice: 'You got to do me one more favour. I want you to go back disguised as Kasajja. Act as he normally does. Do not ask me why because you know the answer.'

A little while later they walked back together. Kawala pretending to be Kasajja chuckled at the food in the same way Kasajja normally did.

Tembo did not take long to realise that it was not Kasajja. At once she complained. 'Douglas, is there anything wrong? Why then have you brought back Kawala instead of Kasajja?'

'Oh I am sorry. I didn't quite realise it. You know these young ones have developed weird tricks. Imagine I had gone to relieve myself. When I returned I thought I was coming with Kasajja. Any way I will go for Kasajja now', Douglas stammered as he explained.

'If that is the problem may be you should leave Kawala here', suggested Tembo.

'Oh no, there is no need for such. I can't accept it because I know you deserve your rest. Kawala may have a good appetite but I will not allow her to finish the best part of the food before Kasajja arrives', Douglas argued. He looked at Kawala and winked his eye beckoning her to leave. She left without word. Again as soon as they were out of Tembo's sight, Douglas turned to Kawala in a sweet singsong voice. I guess it is your lucky day. So be prepared for another round. I hope there is still room in that belly of yours.

'There is a lot more than you can imagine, Uncle Douglas. I mean who wouldn't afford space with all that rich food? Besides you have no choice', chuckled Kawala in a clearly sarcastic way.

'Come off it Kawala! Of course I have all the choices in the world', Douglas protested.

'You surely don't want me to tell my mother about the bone.'

Kawala had hardly completed her statement when Douglas broke in. 'Oh no no! You dare not because if you do, you will lose the best. You know I always reserve the best for my friends.' He started to pat the little elephant on the trunk. Then he whispered something into her ear. Suddenly he started to speak again pretending to be addressing Kasajja. 'You there, get up. Kasajja! Wake up. It is dinner time. Boy! You ought to see what your mother brought home today. It is simply too good to miss. Come on! Get up. As for you Kawala, don't try to trick me again.' Once again Douglas the Dog walked back with Kawala.

Tembo immediately protested. 'I am their mother and can tell my calves even without looking. That one with you is the same one who was here before. That is Kawala.' She rose up. 'Uncle Douglas, since you seem to be failing may be I better lend a hand.'

Douglas was quick to avert the situation using all kinds of words he could think off. 'I am sorry. This time I thought I had brought Kasajja. May be my eyes are not as good as they should be. Anyway you need not worry because I am going to hold Kasajja with my own paws before we set out. In any case you are tired and need some rest. If I fail this time then I will give up.'

Once again Douglas the Dog went and did exactly the same thing. He returned with Kawala. This time, Tembo for her part was not willing to give him another chance. She screamed at the top of her voice. 'Uncle Douglas, you are up to something. I told you to bring the other calf but instead you keep bringing the same one again and again. Enough is enough. I will go there myself.'

As Tembo rose to go, Douglas began to prepare for the race of his life. He held his head low and tucked the tail between the legs as he counted his steps to the perimeter of their homestead. He stopped a short distance away to watch Tembo.

Tembo entered Kasajja's pen, 'Kasajja, what are you playing at? It is dinner time. She extended her trunk to touch him only to be greeted by a swarm of flies.' Her heart missed a beat. 'Flies? I hope it is not what I am thinking.' She touched him again but there was no reaction. 'Let you not be dead I pray because if you are I will kill Douglas myself', she yelled in alarm. She tried to roll him over but that was when she noticed how cold and stiff his body was. 'It can't be true. I will take him out where I can see the problem myself', she said as she lifted Kasajja. With outside light she could just about make out everything. Just above the eye was a sore gone septic, with hundreds of maggots at work. 'Oh no! My Kasajja is dead', she cried. 'He has a sceptic sore above the eye. This is strange. How come I did not see that before I left?' With her trunk she blew away the maggots. 'This sore must have caused by something sharp. Was he involved in a fight? If so that would mean Uncle Douglas left them to roam about in the forest. Was he shot with a poisoned arrow?' She turned to Kawala who had been standing by. 'Kawala you are going to tell me everything that happened here. Tell me right now or else you too will be as dead as your brother.'

'Nothing happened' Kawala answered nervously. Her eyes peered towards Douglas who by now was hiding behind a bush outside the homestead.

'Did Uncle Douglas let you wander about in the forest?'
'No mother.'

'Did Douglas hurt Kasajja? I want the truth because so far it is clear that you planned everything with Douglas. You killed Kasajja so that you could eat all the food alone.' Her ears rattled as she spoke. 'I am not going to let you eat the food that I laboured to bring. No it won't happen. I know just what to do with you. I will break all your legs and leave you to die a very slow death', Tembo fumed. 'I will sit hear watching flies eat you.'

The force of Tembo's voice was enough to scare even the toughest creature in the forest. Kawala began to shake. And just about then Tembo swung her trunk and struck Kawala on the back. The pain spread throughout the body. There is no room for such pain Kawala told herself. By now tears filled her eyes. 'Mother it wasn't me. It was Uncle Douglas. He was eating bones. One hit Kasajja's head but he did not kill him. I am sure Kasajja died in his sleep.'

From his hideout Douglas the Dog heard the result of mother daughter interrogation. He carefully started to crawl further away from the homestead.

Meanwhile Tembo went on screaming. 'It was Douglas. I knew it. I always knew he was up to no good. I will kill him for this.' She rushed out. 'Douglas! Where are you?' she yelled out.

Douglas was already on the move. Tail between the legs and ears pointed forward, he ran for his life. Tembo tried to give a chase but with all her weight, she could not come anywhere close. She gave up and returned home to mourn her calf. The other elephants in the forest joined her for the funeral.

# Chapter 3

Tembo never really recovered from the loss of her calf. She could not stop blaming herself for what happened. 'I was the one who built up that pile of bones and I was also the one who trusted Douglas', she told herself. 'If I had not done so my Kasajja would still be alive. I will never let such a thing happen again.' She set fire on the bones.

Tembo's misfortune provoked the rest of the elephant family to convene a meeting. There in the meeting they concluded a set of rules to govern their life style. It was agreed that from hence no elephant would ever eat meat again. They were to survive on grass, tree leaves, fruits and shrubs. They also recommended that each nursing mother would look after her own calf until they were big enough to fend for themselves. Even then they would still stick with the herd. That is why to date mother elephants never really wander far away from their young and must often be seen walking with them.

Days and nights went by with no sign of Douglas the Dog. Tembo kept burning with rage. And she never gave up trying to find ways of catching Douglas. One day as she lay about an idea came to her mind. She felt happy about it and began to talk aloud. 'Douglas the Dog may run but he can never hide forever. There must be a way of getting him round.' She paused and decided to roll and wallow in excitement. She stopped and resumed her monologue. 'I think I know how to flash him out of his hideout. As I live I will get that Douglas here. Then and only then will I exact my revenge. I can't wait to squash those bones of his.' She grinned. 'I am just going to capitalise on his weakness. I know he never likes to miss parties, so I will organise one. Yes, I am going to throw a party for all animals of the forest. It will be a big one. Oh no. Not just a big one but also the biggest ever to be held in the forest. There will be good music. No, not good but the best music. The champion dancer Remy the Sheep will be there too. And the food shall be as never seen before. I shall make its aroma fill the entire forest. Then I will wait to see if Douglas the Dog can resist it.' She kept quiet and went on with her mental preparations.

Soon, word went round to all animals about the planned party. Douglas the Dog too, heard of it but simply wondered what he would do. Certainly he could not afford to miss it. Yet at the same time he had reason to fear. He had caused the death Tembo's calf. He racked his mind trying to find a way. Several days later having given up all hope of going to the party, he decided to visit Remy the Ram. He found Remy too engrossed in his costume making to notice his presence. He coughed to clear his voice just to draw attention. When he realised that Remy was not quite amused he started to talk. 'I suppose you will be going to the party.'

'Naturally, as you know it is such occasions that bring my fame as a dancer to the foreground. I won the dancing contest and I intend to be the champion for the rest of my days', Remy the Sheep explained rather boastfully.

'Lucky for some, I wish I could be there too. I mean, at least I could see what happens and besides there would always be free food', Douglas remarked.

'I pray you are not foolish enough to go there because Tembo would skin you alive' bleated Remy as he carefully put his costume away.

'I know that and precisely that is why I cannot appear there. I guess it was my fault', Douglas began but was interrupted by Remy.

'Sure enough it was your fault. You were the very one who promised never to eat bones. If you want my opinion I should say you made a stupid promise. In future you should contact others before you agree to something that will most likely bind you for the rest of your life. Learn from us sheep. Our golden rule is: *Never promise what you know you will not fulfil.*'

'I guess you are right but it is too late now', said Douglas repentantly. Since he arrived he had not sat down. He was simply pacing up and down. Now all of a sudden he stopped with eyes fixed on Remy. He burst into laughter. 'May be I can after all come to that party. I think I have found the answer', he said excitedly.

'What are you talking about? Going to Tembo's party? Douglas, you are the maddest dog in the entire forest.' Remy remarked unable to hide his concern for a friend.

Douglas the Dog continued beckoning for calm. 'Just calm down while I explain it.' He said it so sweetly and convincingly that Remy immediately cocked his tiny ears to listen.

Douglas went on. 'Look at your hairy body! Look at your tail, thick enough to cover almost anything any size.

Remy broke in protesting. 'You are not thinking of getting me involved. Oh no! Do not even think of it. You expect me to cover you? Forget it. Pretend that we did not even talk about it.'

'Well, I thought you were my friend. I think I was wrong. I am just a dog with no friends. It is my fault.' Douglas was playing his words to suite the occasion. 'I guess I blew it. If only I had not eaten that bone, I would still be having one friend. Now I am alone with no one to turn to.' Douglas was now in tears.

'Don't be silly! I am still your friend. The only problem is that you are putting my whole life at stake. You want to destroy me, let alone my career.'

'In short you are trying to say that you can't afford to make sacrifices for a friend', interjected Douglas.

Remy did not comment. He had relapsed to daydreaming of some sort. His silence made Douglas the Dog feel even more uncomfortable. He was about to open his mouth when Remy started to speak. 'Oh yes, that new costume could easily do the job. Bedecked in it I would emerge pretending to be applying new dance steps and tricks. Yes, those slow but articulate moves that leave everyone staring and desiring more. Imagine all ewes bleating my name!'

Douglas couldn't make head or tail of Remy's rumbling. 'What are you on about? Have you gone crazy?' asked Douglas anxiously.

Remy made a short but loud burst of laughter after which he remarked sarcastically; 'Look at this! How ironic! The guy I want to help thinks I am crazy. Remy is not. He is only using his brains to search ways of helping some friend who is mad about parties.'

'I suppose you don't mean me? Come on then! Tell me what you have in mind', Douglas pleaded.

'I think I can help you after all. I will design my dancing costume in such a way that I can hide you in it. Of course I may have to sacrifice my dancing agility but for the benefit of a friend in danger of being slain I think I can risk it. For my part, I have considered the dangers involved in this plan of mine. They are many and may even entail sacrificing the beauty of the forest. But such is life. One has to be willing to make sacrifices.' He threw his costume to the nearby hammock. 'I am sure we can still survive outside the forest.'

Douglas beamed with a smile wagging his tail excitedly. 'You are incredibly kind. I do not know how to repay you for your goodness.'

Remy decided it was time to introduce some joke into the discussion. 'You may be excited about hiding your head under my tail but be warned it will not be that comfortable. Besides, underneath you are bound to discover a lot of unpleasant truth about sheep especially after they have had a good meal. You know good food means a lot of unpleasant winds. I suppose you can endure it as reparation for your misdeed.'

'I read you. So it is all about enduring the stench emitted from your rear. Imagine I have to eat my food surrounded by your exhaust fumes. I think I am really crazy.'

'You mean you didn't know?' Remy Joked.

They both laughed at the joke. Remy continued explaining the details of the plan including contingencies. That evening, Douglas the Dog returned to his hideout caught himself a fowl for dinner. Then he crawled to the hollow underneath of an ancient thorny tree with a big smile on his face. He was after all going to the party. He lay in waiting for sleep which didn't want to come. Meanwhile his mind wandered about reliving his experiences. When he lived with Tembo he never had to work to get food. At first he pretended to ignore it but the fact that he did not have the freedom to hunt as and when he wanted to, made him realise his mistake. There were times when, instead of catching his prey he had had to lay low because he could see a herd of elephants nearby. He finally closed his eyes and dreamt about nothing else but Tembo's party.

# Chapter 4

The special day finally came. It was party day thanks to Tembo the Elephant. All animals in their various capacities assembled at the Elephant court. Remy the Sheep, the champion dancer of the forest too arrived in style. His specially designed costume attracted everyone's attention and he decided he would enjoy it as he made his way to his seat, which by special request was in isolation from other animals just to enable him to concentrate on the new moves.

Soon everything was rolling in party mood. Guests were getting to know each other. Old ones were gossiping and little ones playing round. But Remy the Sheep remained silent. Occasionally he was seen grinning and giggling alone. A few times he mumbled out audibly some words to what others came to think of as an imaginary friend. The more he sat quietly, the more others wondered what he had to hide. Soon his apparent aloofness was challenged by Kiddie the Goat. He approached and addressed Remy: 'Hi Remy! Why seat in isolation? This is not like you?'

'Everyone changes. I just want to be alone. You may want to know that to dance with style you need absolute self-composure. On that note and if you do not mind please leave me alone', said Remy as he waved Kiddie off.

Douglas thought it was funny and from his hideout underneath Remy he remarked, 'That was a beautiful way of getting rid of someone.'

'If I were you I would simply shut up. Have you forgotten that I am missing a lot of fun because of you? Look at even amateurs claiming that they can beat me!' Remy the Sheep was angry. 'The truth is that I am not sure how long I can hold on like this. I have a crown to defend and as king dancer, I should be out there showing off with my attire.'

'All right, I get the message', Douglas whispered back. 'I am sorry for messing your day.'

As the day dragged on Remy the Sheep's behaviour began to provoke more and more suspicion. When food was served he had helped himself to more food than he normally did. Usually he never ate meat but on this particular occasion he demanded it. And what is more, ever since he came to the party he had neither moved nor spoken to other important visitors.

Now even Tembo was suspicious. 'My friend Remy the Sheep must be hiding something of interest. I wouldn't be surprised if Douglas the Dog is not somewhere in the neighbourhood. But I will not disturb him as yet. I will wait to see him dance', she told her elephant friends.

'We will keep an eye on him', replied Nana the Elephant.

'I have an even better idea. Why don't we provoke Remy to dance?'

'May be not yet', said Tembo. 'We will wait for the right time when Remy will be expected to take to centre stage.'

That hour of challenge finally came. Every animal rose to dance leaving the centre for the champion. Much to their surprise Remy the champion's dance left a lot to be desired. Tembo decided it was time to have a word with Remy. She approached and drew his attention. 'Are you all right Remy?'

Remy turned to her careful enough to shield off Douglas from her sight. 'Well, couldn't be better. Thank you', answered Remy.

Tembo went on without arousing interest from the other guests. 'Well then why aren't you dancing to your standard? Can't you see even the poorest dancers are making the better of you? If you don't change your way of dancing maybe I will do something else. Perhaps I will turn this party into a dancing competition. I do not need to remind you that your crown could easily be passed onto someone else.'

Remy protested. 'I am surprised at your behaviour. I thought I was here as your guest, why then do you approach me in that way?'

'Remy you are mistaken. This is my party and I can do with it what I want. Right now I am calling for a dancing competition. I want to see you lose. Actually I will make sure that regardless of what you do, you will be a looser.'

Remy went on. 'I am sorry. I take that as an insult. I demand an apology or else I will leave in protest.'

'Makes no difference to me, Remy or no Remy the dancing competition can go on. And for your own information, as soon as another champion comes on, I will personally strip you of the crown in the most humiliating way ever seen.'

'You are surely joking. Remy the Sheep is a champion and will always be', said Remy.

'Well, I may just take a short cut. I am going to proclaim someone else champion. Kiddie the Goat will be the new champion. I mean there is no need for a contest. It is my party and I dictate what goes on.' She turned around to Remy and with a stern look went on. 'Just one word of advice, I am going to ask you one more time before I proclaim another champion. If you do not dance the way you are expected to, then I will not ask you to leave the party. No. I will personally throw you out. But not without breaking every single bone of yours.'

Remy the Sheep was terrified. He began to imagine his dancing crown on someone else. He thought of the humiliation involved. Then again there was Douglas the Dog whose life was in danger. He thought of his own future. It was a hard decision to call especially as he let feelings come in. Eventually he said to himself: I know Douglas is my friend and I promised to help him but I am just not yet ready to lose my title. Right now I think it is up to him. He looked round as he prepared himself for the champion's jump. He kicked his hind legs on the ground with such enthusiasm that everyone realised the champion was at it again. Then to Tembo he said, 'play the right beat because the champion is back to his domain.'

'Here we go!' screamed Remy. The tempo with which he started to dance shook Douglas so violently that the straps that held his pouch on to Remy broke.

Douglas began to complain. 'Hey mate! I am almost falling. Slow down I beg you.'

Remy ignored Douglas' plea. He started to dance even more vigorously than before jumping higher and higher, hoping from place to place and wriggling from side to side.

Inside the pouch which was his hideout, Douglas the Dog tossed about as Remy danced. At one point he could swear he had hit his head on the ground. He tried to use his paws to tickle Remy but he seemed to make things worse. Suddenly his attention was drawn to the stretching pouch. He wondered how much longer it would hold his weight. Indeed the head was already beginning to peer out as excited Remy swung from side to side.

Once again Douglas pleaded. 'Please, Remy slow down. My head is now visible.' But Remy paid no attention. Instead he was even jumping higher than before. As everyone cheered Remy jumped and somersaulted in the air. This time when he landed on the ground Douglas the Dog fell out of Remy's costume. Although he landed with all force, there was no time to reckon the pain. He immediately rose to his feet and ducking between dancers, he ran for his life. Tembo and her cronies gave chase but by the time they manoeuvred their way through the excited crowd, Douglas had already gained ground. They chased through the forest but all was in vain. Douglas the dog, head down and tail between legs just continued running for his life. He ran out of the forest where he met a man. Douglas stopped his tongue out as he panted for breath but at the same time apprehensive of the creature before him.

The man approached Douglas in a surprisingly friendly way. 'You seem to be running from some kind of danger. What is it?'

'Well, there is someone after my life. It is someone almost a million times my size.'

'Must be really big but all the same you ought to relax.'

'Surely I would love to but what if Tembo the Elephant catches up with me?'

'I guarantee you safety, for out of the forest I, the man I am the king. Yet I must add if you are really scared maybe we can talk inside my dwelling place. We men call our dwelling places houses. You can come to mine, if you choose to.'

'I do not know anything about you but I guess I can trust you. Take me to your house', Douglas requested. 'Hide me there until it is all safe then you can do with me whatever you want. Literally anything provided it does not mean taking me to live in the forest again.'

So it was that man welcomed Douglas the Dog to his house. He sat by the fireplace. The atmosphere was so relaxing that in no time Douglas felt confident enough to tell his story. He kept nothing. At the end of it he waited for the man to judge. It came in the words he least expected. 'This is my house. If you like, feel welcome. Stay as long as you wish. There is no charge for that.'

'Oh, that is very kind of you', said Douglas.

'One more thing', the man went on. 'Here there are no laws about bones. Matter of fact we men are not in the habit of eating bones. Occasionally we may bite off the soft ends but no more. You may eat as many bones as you like', the man added.

'Thank you so much Mr Man. I do not know how to repay you but I will do it in my own way. From now on I will serve you against your enemies and a lot more. I want us to be the best friends ever. I want all generations to know that from now on man's best friend is a dog. Yes, Douglas the Dog, man's best friend.'

'Accepted and consider it a deal', concurred the man.

That was how dogs left the forest and came to live with human being.

Meanwhile Tembo frustrated by failure to catch Douglas the Dog transferred her anger to Remy the Sheep. But once again she was too late. Remy and his team of ewes had run away at about the same time when Douglas set out. Following a different path from the forest he arrived and settled to live with human beings in a large open grassland.

Like Douglas he too pledged servitude to at mankind though at a different level. Unlike Douglas, they would provide humans with not just milk and wool but also mutton.

In return the humans agreed to provide food, water, shelter and medical care if and when needed. They also agreed to protect Remy and his team of ewes from predators like coyotes, bears and eagles that will kill and eat the sheep. The man fenced up the large piece of open grazing land for Remy and his team.

# Phoebe and the Talking Toad

# Phoebe Plans Surprise Meal

Back in the days, there lived, a good-hearted man and his wife in a little village near a big river. They had only one child, a little girl whom they called Phoebe. She was extremely beautiful. Father and mother loved her so dearly that they never wanted anything bad to happen to her. They brought her with them everywhere they went. The only exception was when they went to work in the fields. On such occasions Phoebe stayed at home helping out with little household duties under the watchful eye of the neighbours and indeed everyone in the village who stayed home.

North of the same village, separated only by a wide river there was a forest. Word had it that the forest was inhabited by man-eating wizards and witches. While parents went out to work, these man-eaters too went about hunting for children left alone at home and waylaying those who tried to cross the forest on their own. Phoebe like all the other village children were aware and had been warned about this. As for Phoebe, her parents had instructed her never to wander far from home on her own and if possible to keep in doors.

One day while her parents were gone to work in the fields, Phoebe decided that she would cook something little to eat and some for her parents. Unfortunately for her, there was no fire in the house and she did not know how her mother always made hers any way. Phoebe was not the type of girl who gave up that easily. She had made up her mind to cook and she was going to do it. She began to talk to herself. "I want mother to know that I am a big girl. I am going to cook food enough for all of them so that when they come back they will find everything ready", she told herself. "As for fire, I will just have to get some from the neighbours". She went from house to house in the village but was not successful.

In another village, not far away, she had heard, lived an old woman who always had fire. All housewives whose fire died out went to her for it. Phoebe intent on cooking decided to go to the old woman. 'I know she does not go away from her home so if I go now I am sure I will find her. I must go there and return quickly so as to have everything ready before my parents return', she told herself as she set off. What she did not know was that between her village and that where the old woman lived was a forest where the man-eating warlocks lived.

Phoebe set off hurriedly without rousing attention of the neighbour who was charged with looking after her. On the way she sang and occasionally whistled away the melodies she had learnt from her grandmother. Soon she was at the river that marked the end of her village. She made her way over the single pole bridge without difficulty and was about to run when she heard a voice call her name. She looked around but could see nobody.

Again as she tried to walk a voice called out; 'Phoebe!' She turned around to see who had called her but there was no one. All she could see was a giant toad, a type she had never before seen. She was a little terrified but did not want to show it. Secretly she had made up her mind to run as fast as she could and was just about to do so when the giant toad spoke.

'Little lady! I am the one who called your name. My name is Toad the Amphibian. I am a toad not a frog. You see I am concerned about your safety. I mean you should be at home playing with other children. This place is not safe for you', said the Toad. 'Didn't your parents ever tell you about the man-eating warlocks and witches that live in the forest you are about to enter?'

'Now I recall. They also told me never to talk to strangers.'

'I am sure they did. That is very commendable of them. Under normal circumstances, I wouldn't have bothered but this is a life or death situation. Please I am begging you, turn around and go back home.'

'I will go home but right now I am just going to the old woman on the other side of the forest to collect fire', answered Phoebe still amazed that she had seen a Toad that could talk. 'I will be quick and before you know I will be back.'

'Well, I know that but it is too risky for you to go there alone. The man-eating warlocks and witches are very active in that forest. One of them might make an easy picking of you'. He made a rather strange croaking noise to clear his voice. 'Surely you do not want to become some wizard's dinner', explained the Toad.

'Oh no, they won't and can never catch me. I can run very fast. If you should know, I am the fastest girl in the whole of our village. Besides I am a strong girl.' She started showing off her biceps. 'I make sure that I eat all my dinners and all my vegetables and fruits.' She made a fist out of her hand. 'You see the muscles coming?'

'Think again little girl. Go back home and wait for your parents', advised Toad. 'You don't want to put pain into hearts of those who cherish you.'

'Well, big frog,' she started but was rudely interrupted.

'I am not a frog. I am a toad.'

'Sorry about that but to me you are just like a frog except may be for the colour and the rough skin. I have a plan in mind and you are wasting my time. I want to surprise my parents. I want them to find food ready when they come back from the fields. Now I should be going. Whoever you are, just do not make me waste any more time. Good day mister Frog'.

'Mr Toad', the toad completed her statement. 'I am called Toad the Amphibian. As I said before I am a toad, not a frog. I would be honoured if you maintained that distinction.' He watched as Phoebe, intent on doing her own stuff stared on.

'As I was saying', he continued. 'I am a toad and this river is my home although time and again I go to the forest to search of some grub. Of course there is plenty in the water as well but sometimes one has to change diet. When I am tired of sea worms and insects, I hop and hop until I am deep in the forest. There is quite plenty for a toad to eat out there.' He rolled his eyes back and forth and his tongue popped out too. He croaked a little as though to draw attention then he resumed his talk. 'We are talking here about those large and juicy insects of the forest. For your information that is why I often gate crash into bonfire parties in your village. And while I am there in the forest I observe a lot of what happens.'

Phoebe was losing patience and couldn't hide any more. 'Why am I wasting my time with a talking frog or toad?' asked Phoebe. Then as though she remembered something turned towards the toad with an unusually assertive tone of speech. 'Mister Talking Toad, if it is true that you go to the forest every now and then, why doesn't the wizard eat you?'

Toad rolled his eyes as he prepared to respond. 'The answer is as simple as a toad swimming. The wizard is a man-eater. He eats human beings. Toad the Amphibian is not human. Therefore he is no food to the wizard. Besides I am kind of special. He dare not mess with me.'

'What about the grown up humans? Why don't they eat them? Queried Phoebe.

'That would be the best question to ask those cannibals. My guess is that they are interested in young flesh because it is better than sinewy one from grown-ups.'

Phoebe had just about had enough. 'Thanks for your advice but I really have to get the fire. I will see you on my way back', she said as she briskly walked away.

Toad tried in vain to call her back but Phoebe had already run away. She disappeared into the forest. Toad dived into the water thinking hard about what to do. Much as he knew this was his time to make an impression on the family of this girl. He pictured the times he had been maltreated by children at bonfires and wondered if this was not his chance to put it right. Maybe if he did something really remarkable they would start to accept him in their families. He soon found himself at the bank of the river at the edge of the forest but with no solution to his problems. In the end he said resignedly. 'I will wait right here and if I do not see her then I will have to go to the forest to rescue her.' He smiled as a feeling of bravado coursed through his blood vessels. 'Those humans will be proud of my achievement when they see what I have done.' He stopped talking to himself and just croaked away like all toads. He started talking to himself again as past memories filled his head. 'Am I stupid or what? What makes me think that those humans will want to change their attitude towards me? Take for instance at bonfires. Why do they have to be so mean? All

I want is to help myself to some bugs attracted by the light but you find someone wanting to make a football out of me. What a mean species humans are! I will do it anyway because I like Phoebe.' He hopped onto a stone and sat their waiting.

# Phoebe and the Man-eater wizard

The Man-eater wizard was hiding in a tree not far from the old woman's hut. Matter of fact that was his usual place where he caught his unsuspecting victims. When he saw Phoebe he prepared to capture her. She was right under the tree when he grabbed her from the back. Before she could scream, her head was already inside a giant pumpkin that muffled any sounds she made. With a strong bark cloth, he wrapped on his back. He hitched a ride from a whirl wind to the heart of the forest where he lived.

Back in the safety of the forest, the wizard unwrapped his picking of the day. He put a chain round the ankle and fastened the rest round a big stone. Finally he removed the pumpkin from her head. Seeds and gooey mouldering pumpkin flesh was all over her head. Phoebe started to wipe the pumpkin off her face.

'Sorry for being a poor host', the wizard said. 'I have just what you need to clean that face of yours.' He pulled out a filthy piece of cloth from under his tunic. He shook off the maggots and fly pupae. The stench was so strong that Phoebe almost threw up. The wizard spat a giant phlegm on the cloth. 'This will do the job', he said as he held out to Phoebe.

Eww yuck! 'No thank you. That cloth is too filthy for my face. I can manage without it.' She started wiping her face with her finger.

The wizard rolled his eyes in anger. 'You want to use your hands? Go ahead'. Almost instantly Phoebe's hands spread wide like a scarecrow. The rest of the body apart from the head which could still be moved around, went stiff. He shook the dirty cloth under Phoebe's chin. 'That will take care of any unnecessary screaming and foul language.' Then he threw a calabash of ice cold water over her face. 'There you are. No more muck on your face.'

Phoebe cried out. 'Why are you doing this to me?'

'Call it preparing my dinner. Why do you think I snatched you? You are going to be my dinner. But first I must show you my castle.' He swung his wand round while uttering some incomprehensible spells.

Overwhelmed by fear and regrets, Phoebe wasn't really listening. She had closed her eyes and thought of the toad whose admonition she had ignored. At the time it had seemed a joke being advised by a despicable creature that she could easily hold in the palm of her arm. Amidst the silence of regrets tears washed down her cheeks. She opened her eyes just in time when, with rumbling and peels of lightning the wizard's castle appeared. The massive cobwebs and the adorning skulls, skeletons and floating maggot infested cauldrons made it extremely eerie. The air smelt like decaying flesh. Phoebe would probably have passed out if it had not been for the aching limbs caused by the scarecrow posture she had been magically committed to.

'So what do you think of my humble abode?'

'I refuse to answer until you free my hands.'

'Oh sorry. I forgot about that.' He pointed his wand towards her and the induced paralysis vanished. 'Move them up and down to restore the blood flow. Don't try to be clever as to escape. Nobody ever gets away from my fortress alive except when I want to use them to feed my pet pythons.' He hardly finished his sentence when a big snake slithered by expectantly. 'Python don't scare our guest. Disappear', he commanded. As the python disappeared into the woods he continued. 'Sit on that log. You will be safe there until dinner time.'

The politeness in Phoebe was on the automatic. 'Thank you Mr Wizard', she said.

Shocked by the kind response the wizard, lifted his face gear and smiled. 'Thank you child.' His voice sounded civil. 'My name in Dark Thunder. I guess that explains the darkness that shrouds my home.

'You have got a cool name'.

The wizard responded with a truly thunder like voice. 'It is not meant to be cool. It is meant to be scary.'

'I am sorry. I meant to say very scary and cool at the same time. That is the way kids in the village would describe it.'

'Are there many kids in your village?' the wizard asked.

'I refuse to answer.'

'Well be my guest. It doesn't really bother me knowing that I have enough food to look after me. Soon all that will be left of you will be just bones.'

Even in the midst of fear Phoebe managed to summon up some courage to ask the wizard questions. In fact it was her way of handling the fear. 'Where is the rest of your family?'

'Why do you ask?'

'Just curious'.

'Keep it that way. Call it the curiosity of someone going to be eaten soon by a family of wizards unless of course I change my mind.'

'I am not scared of you. Besides I am sure very soon my parents come searching for me.'

'Dream on girl. How will they ever find you?'

'I don't know but they will. Think of it this way, everyone in the village knows about man-eaters like you who live in this forest. You should be scared that village witch doctors might just use their spells to find me.'

'I did think about that too. And if you must know my little errand is to invite my friends for dinner.' He held Phoebe by the chin. 'I think you make good kebab. I can't wait seeing your little body roasting away on wood fire.'

Fear coursed through her spine and tears flowed involuntarily. For once Phoebe had to admit the evil creature before her meant what he said. She was crying out loud but with no sound.

As for the wizard, he had his own plans. Usually the Man-eater wizard never wasted time with his victims. He ate them up as soon as he got them. Not so with Phoebe any way. Her beauty captured his attention so much such that he decided to keep her as his pet and slave. He mumbled some spell. Instantly Phoebe was tied on to some sort of rocking chair with gags on her mouth. 'You will be safe here until I get back. Got some business to take care of. Cock-a-doodle-doo, my cockerel will keep an eye on you while I am gone. He is good at his job and will alert me as soon as something starts to happen'.

By now Phoebe was rocking frantically and making mumbling noises.

The wizard loosened the gags. 'Now what is it that you want to say?'

'Surely you are not going to leave me alone in the heart of the forest tied to the chair'. She cried out.

'This is safe. Besides Cock-a-doodle-doo, there is an army of zombies at my disposal. I can summon them to guard you.'

The picture of real zombies teeming round her was indeed scary given that she used to freak out whenever her mother tuned on to the walking dead zombie show. She had to think real fast. 'Sir Mr Wizard. There is no need to summon zombies. I was just thinking of something that I could do while you are gone? Something like watch the TV.' The hindsight realisation that she was in the forest where there was no electricity made her close her eyes as she silently went through a tirade of obscenities. 'Never mind the TV, I just want something to keep me busy and entertained before I face my demise.'

'Very well then, there is a host of wizard entertainment.' Dark Thunder swung his wand and a calabash came floating in the air and stationed itself before Phoebe. Dark Thunder uttered a mouthful of spell and watched as the calabash bowl levelled up just the right distance from Phoebe. The angle of vision was incredibly perfect. 'Now you have the viewing bowl. I guess you will need some form of gizmo to operate the entertainment bowl.' Out of nowhere came what looked like a skink lizard. 'This will allow you to change the channels. Press the pattern or colour to access what you need. Press the head to increase the volume and press the tail to lower it.'

Phoebe watched with fear mixed with admiration. The curiosity in her was querying how the device worked. She even thought it would be something cool and worthwhile introducing to their village.

'One more move', yelled the wizard. At that point Phoebe's hands were freed but the legs seemed to have acquired a complete different burden. 'I have tied a big rock to your legs. The only way you can escape from it is by cutting off the legs. And if you decided to run, well then you will a big load to drag along. You won't go far and you certainly wouldn't hide because the trail will lead me to right where you are.'

Tears of regret and helplessness welled up. 'Why are you torturing me? Just kill me and get it done with.' Phoebe cried.

'I have to follow special rituals. In the meantime since you wanted entertainment, there it is. Your control is here' he said as he placed the skink lizard in her hand.

'Take away your stupid lizard. I don't like lizards. I am afraid of them.' Phoebe flung off the lizard and watched make its way back.

'Well, it won't leave you alone. My advice is that get used to it. As for me and myself, we are out of here. Business awaits. See you before dark.' With that, Dark Thunder vanished leaving Phoebe wondering how he had done that. The skink lizard meanwhile station itself in her palm.

# Mr Toad the Amphibian's Rescue Package

Toad waited on the same spot he had met Phoebe. It turned out to be one of his best days as far as food was concerned. Ever since he sat there he had lost count of the insects he had eaten. He was already full up now and was just basking about in the sun. As time went by he did not see Phoebe return to her home and was disturbed. He knew at once that she could have fallen victim to the wizard. He decided he would be the one to rescue her. He went to the forest on a scouting mission and was glad to see Phoebe alive although still captive. He thought of ways of helping her but none seemed to come. Eventually he decided to creep through a crevice in the wall of the hut where Phoebe was held captive. He did not have to worry about being seen because his colour just about blended in with the wall. He looked round to ascertain that there was nobody else in the room. In an extra low croak he drew her attention to his whereabouts. 'I want you to listen very carefully', he said. 'I am going to look for help. Do you understand?'

Phoebe nodded in consent. 'In the meantime, don't do anything silly.'

'Okay frog', said Phoebe.

'I am a toad, not a frog. I am out of here and will soon be back with the necessary help.

Phoebe watched the toad crawl through the hole in the wall and then as he hopped his way into the forest, she did not know whether to believe him and wait or try to work out her own escape plan. Already she had sourced out that if she behaved well, there was a fair chance she would win the wizards trust then and only then would she make her escape.

Meanwhile Toad the Amphibian spent lots of time scouting all possible routes. The shortest of them had lots of hardships which had to be overcome if one had to go through successfully. It involved crossing the river at the broadest and deepest point. He smiled and told himself, 'This is the point where Toad the Amphibian will become useful. I will help her cross the river. I mean I will swim her across.' His eyes rolled in their sockets as if he had seen an enemy but he was not. He was simply overjoyed at his own plan. Once again he burst into monologue. 'Imagine Toad the Amphibian swimming across with the little girl on her back. What a crazy idea! Her foot alone cannot rest on my back and if at all it did, I couldn't balance that weight let alone swim without sinking.' He made a loud croak. 'Let's pretend that I was strong enough and that she could stand on my back! I wonder how the poor wizard would react when he sees me swimming with her on my back! He would probably try to kill her. He may even aim at her with a spear.' Suddenly his face started to droop. 'On dear, then I would have led her to her death.'

He tried to think of an alternative ways with closed eyes but had to open them as a fly flew by. He grabbed it with his tongue. 'Well, that was really tasty. Pity they always come when one is already full up. But I can always squeeze room for one more', said Toad delighted at his catch.

As though the fly he had just eaten had given him insight he gaped his mouth in smile saying; 'I think I know just what to do. I will swallow her up then I will swim across the river with her in my belly. I will hop all the way to her parents' home and spew her there.' Suddenly he burst into laughter. 'Now that is what I call a stupid idea. How on earth can I swallow such a big girl? That is impossible.' He began to chant loud 'impossible! Impossible! I cannot do it. She is several times bigger than me.'

Theo the Tortoise had swum and settled just a few feet from Toad. He had listened to his ranting. When Toad stopped Theo joined in 'that was very impressive. I only wish you had music to those words. I bet a simple croak would have made all the difference.'

'What are you talking about?' Toad asked.

'Oh, recently I started a new career. I want to be a singing tortoise. Soon this whole river shall be filled with sweet melodies from the tortoise choir. Isn't that sweet? Then we can actually put music to your own words. What a thrill that will be!' rattled Theo.

'I am a little busy right now and I am sure I would do well with a bit of silence round me', Toad the Amphibian retorted.

'That much I know. Let's say Theo the tortoise is here to solve your problem. I mean I am here to solve what you call impossible.' Toad watched with spite as Theo crawled out of water. Happily perched on a dry piece of land Theo started to talk. He hardly gave Toad chance to say anything. 'That girl of yours we can still save her. You can do it provided he has not made a meal of her yet.'

Toad suddenly couldn't ignore Theo's presence any more. With his mind on overdrive he began to think of how he could save her. Was Theo going to help him or was there another way. 'How can we save her?' asked Toad.

'That is pretty easy. You are going to do exactly what you decided before. You will swallow her. That is how you will save her', explained Theo.

'But that is impossible', ejaculated Toad.

'Oh no, it is not. Come with me and I will show you something.' Theo and Toad swam right to the bottom of the river. There at the riverbed a team of tortoises and turtles gathered singing. Their voices sweetly covered the riverbed. Toad watched with admiration.

'You mean tortoises actually do sing? That is incredible. I love it', croaked Toad.

'Now you see for yourself that nothing is really impossible. Just as tortoises can sing so too can toads swallow what seems too big. Come and meet my friend. I am sure he will help you.'

They came to a rock at the bottom of the sea. Toad followed Theo as he glided round the rock. Suddenly they were surrounded by swarms of snakes.

'Now I get it' said Toad resignedly. 'You brought me here to be someone's dinner. How foolish I was to trust a tortoise! Anyone, whose dinner am I?' Toad cried out.

'Relax! No one is going to eat anyone.'

The toad was nervous. 'I suppose you are talking that way because the creator provided you with natural armour against the serpents. As far as I know snakes love frogs and toads. I am going to close my eyes. Tell whoever it is, to swallow me right now.'

'Welcome to the world where the impossible become possible', a voice roared and just then a big snake crawled close to Toad the Amphibian. 'I am Sleazy the river snake. As your friend Theo the Tortoise must have told you, I help others to realise their dreams. There is nothing too great for me. Nothing is impossible. Now let's hear your story.'

'You mean you are not going to eat me?' queried the Toad.

'Not right now. But maybe one day' Sleazy the Snake replied. 'As I said before, there is nothing impossible.'

Toad the Amphibian rolled his eyes wondering how long he had before he became someone's dinner. 'Very well Mr Sleazy whoever you are. I would like to make one wish before I end up in someone's' belly.'

'Come on Toad. Chillax. What is it that you want?'

Toad was still frightened but something urged him to speak out his story. 'My fascination with humans began when I was a little tadpole. I very much wanted to be with them. When I became a fully-grown toad, I was happy to learn that I was actually capable of living on both land and water. One day with my friends we hopped our way to a nearby home of humans. The entire family was gathered around a bonfire. I must say the fire attracted quite a good many insects. What an easy prey for us! Things seemed okay until a little boy saw my friends and I. He did not say a word. He simply started to kick us about. Off to the air his mighty kick would drive one. That boy! I will never forget him. He seemed to have his own ways of measuring where a toad would fall next, for just then he would swing his foot lifting you even higher. Boy what a fall that was!' Toad the Amphibian went on narrating his feelings.

'I have no grudge against mankind. They still fascinate me and I want to get to know them even more. As far as I know my chance for that has come.' Toad was actually shedding tears but being in water no one could see it. 'I have to rescue that girl from the wizard. The only way I can do that is by carrying her in my belly.'

'The other problem is that you are too small. You ought to be big and much more elastic', Sleazy the snake broke in. 'If you had been a snake, things would have been much easier. But that said we can still do something. Here we make wishes come true. Now close your eyes and make a wish.'

Toad closed his eyes wishing very much to be Phoebe's rescuer. When he opened his eyes he had turned into a giant toad. He was very much overjoyed. 'Thank you very much, Sleazy. And you too, Theo. Now I can go and rescue that girl.'

'Not as you are for she would get frightened', explained Theo. 'You need something that really makes you feel real. I am thinking of you keeping your size and then we would do something to miniaturise the girl.'

'Master, just help me rescue that girl', cried the toad.

'Your wish will be granted. You will return to your usual size. You are a toad and toads do not grow too big.'

Toad the Amphibian blew a bubble of air in water to show his frustration. 'I do not think we are going anywhere. No one seems to understand me. That is a fact', fumed Toad. 'For your own information I did not want to come here. That Theo the tortoise dragged me here. But then again what right do I have to get angry? I am the one who needs help not you. Well, I should be going now. Thanks for your help.'

'Where do you think you are going now?' asked Sleazy the River snake.

'I am going to rescue the poor girl. I have wasted enough time with you. So long friends', he started to swim away but the snake threw his tail and dragged him back.

'What good is your effort alone? Ask yourself, if you were able to how come you haven't saved her up to now?' Sleazy the snake hissed.

'I am still working at it.' Toad the Amphibian realised how correct Sleazy was. He did not need to hurry. 'I am sorry', he croaked.

'Good, then you can wait a little longer. Just sit back and relax. Right now your problem is mine. I have millions of solutions to your problems but the question is choosing the best.'

'May be if you shared the different ideas with us, we could come up with the right one. We could all sit down and discuss these methods. Yes, let's try them', suggested Theo.

Sleazy's eyes shone as he spoke. 'The question is not about being right but choosing the correct method for the given scenario.'

'You guys have totally lost me', murmured the toad.

'Don't worry', said Sleazy. 'We will solve your problem. You just ought to realise that in life, all methods are right but they may not necessarily be correct. Our task here is to choose the correct method. So, shall we sit down? I have presentation to make.'

After several hours Sleazy the magic maker came up with a correct solution. It was decided that Toad retained his size. He was simply given the power to miniaturise and restore to normal anything he wished. Everyone was happy for Toad. They sang and danced round and round, as the tortoise choir raised their voices in joy. It was a joyous moment. Then just as everyone was planning to go away, they noticed that Mr Toad was not happy. His face was drooping. Theo the Tortoise turned to Mr Toad. 'Now what next? Did you have to spoil the lovely moment with your sadness?'

'I am sorry but I can't help it. Look at it this way, you lot have been good to me. You have given me everything I need to save the little girl. Well, not really everything.'

'What is missing?' asked Sleazy.

'Well, you forgot that my life is dinner to others. Not just snakes but also birds of the air. Think of the forest owls and bats! They are always lurking about in wait for me. I do not want to be eaten with the little girl in me. At least on my own I wouldn't worry much.'

'Well spoken, Mr Toad. I think Sleazy the Magician can put that right too', said the river snake smilingly. 'I am going to give you additional powers for you own safety.' He stretched out his tail and tapped the toad on the head. 'That should take care of it. If anyone tries to harm you, you will immediately turn into a stone.'

Mr Toad grinned in smile. 'I think I like that. No more shall Phoebe's cousins kick me about.' He turned to the rest of the team. 'Friends, I will never forget this day. You are true friends. As soon as my mission is finished I will be right here to thank you and to return the powers.'

Toad left the riverbed extremely happy. He swam as fast as he could and was ready to embark on his rescue mission. Unfortunately, a short distance away he got swallowed by a diving pelican before he could use his spell to turn into stone. He kicked about in vain.

The pelican went right into the heart of the forest where Phoebe was imprisoned by the wizard. There in his nest he spewed out the toad. As Toad the Amphibian gathered his breath, the pelican spoke out. 'I am El Pelicano at your service. I was summoned to help you because you are running out of time for the mission.'

'You mean I am not dead yet?'

'I don't think you would be talking if you were dead. Anyway, several feet below this very tree is the subject. She is tied to the chair.'

'How do I untie her with my flimsy toes?' Toad the Amphibian asked.

'Will power can do anything. Besides what you imagine becomes real. Now hop into me my beak. I will fly you down when the time is right.'

'What are you saying?' Toad croaked.

'I am saying. It is change of plan because right now the wizard and his team are back. So we stay put. I will update you because I can see everything down there. Call it aerial surveillance.'

'It is already evening and her parents must be frantically looking for her. We have to do something.'

'Nothing you do now will help. Just stay put and hope that she doesn't get eaten. In the meantime I could use your help. Call it your contribution for being a lodger in my nest.''

'What do you want me to do?'

'Eat up the bugs that are infesting my nest.'

Toad the Amphibian glanced at the bird poo infested with maggots and quickly protested. 'That is your poo.'

'I know, it is just part of the food chain' El Pelicano replied.

# Phoebe's Escape

Being a wizard's captive was the worst punishment that Phoebe was ever to endure. Every day the wizard would come with weird stuff including an occasional cadaver for his dinner. He would dish out some chunks of flesh to Phoebe commanding her to eat but never did she ever accept it. Instead she would cry saying 'if you want you can kill me but I am not going to eat human flesh.' The wizard would not do so for he was too fascinated by her beauty. In fact he felt he would have to look after her well. So it was then that he started bringing her the kind of food she liked fruits, fish and an odd fowl here and again. In return Phoebe asked to be allowed to do some chores around the house. The wizard was delighted with her request. From thence he stopped tying her onto a chair while he went out. Phoebe would wander around the compound and prepare her own dinner.

All days of searching proved fruitless. And as weeks went by without any sign of Phoebe, her parents concluded that she had been eaten by the man-eating wizard. They mourned her and decided to burn whatever reminded them of her.

For her part Phoebe secretly vowed to escape. She never stopped thinking of the troubles her parents were probably going through and was even more determined to escape. True enough she had all the time. Each time the wizard went hunting she was left alone with his special pet rooster that spied and reported everything to him. Phoebe did not know it.

One day Phoebe was all set to go and just as she was about to enter the woods Cock-Doodle-doo the rooster flew to the roof of the hut and started to crow: 'Cock-doodle-Dee Phoebe is escaping'.

She rushed back and sat down with berries in her hands. The wizard on hearing the cockcrow came running home. 'So you were trying to escape?' he asked.

Phoebe denied it saying: 'How can I escape when I don't know where to go?'

'But my rooster never lies. It must have seen you', insisted the wizard. Phoebe denied it again and again. 'May be it thought I was escaping because I was picking these berries.' The wizard believed her and went back to his duty. Immediately Phoebe got up and tried her chance once again. No sooner had he reached than the rooster started to crow again: 'Cock-doodle-Dee Phoebe is escaping'.

Again the wizard came running. This time he found Phoebe holding dry twigs in her hands. 'So what is going on here?'

'I was just gathering twigs to light the fire with', replied Phoebe.

'Trying to cover your escape in that way?' the wizard inquired.

'I have already told you that I cannot escape because I do not know how to get home. Besides I am happy here. There is a lot of food.' She faked tears. If you are fed up of me, please let me know' she cried.

'No I am not. If I were I should have eaten you already', replied the wizard as he returned to his duties in the forest.

The sun was already overhead and Phoebe decided she would not attempt to escape again until the next day. When the next day she tried it, the rooster kept crowing and the wizard kept coming back. Each time the wizard came back he would find Phoebe either gathering twigs or simply sitting in the sun. Phoebe could not escape on the second day either.

On the third day she was determined to escape. So as soon as the wizard left she also set off. But she couldn't get anywhere as the rooster kept crowing to alert the wizard of her moves. When the rooster crowed during her second attempt, the wizard who had had to abandon whatever he had been up to, was very cross with the rooster. He rushed home but instead of questioning Phoebe, he grabbed the rooster, killed it and ordered Phoebe to cook it. She was ever so delighted to put the rooster into an earth pot to cook. Meanwhile the wizard went back to his hunting. This time he promised Phoebe that he would not come back until late.

Phoebe was glad for now she could escape. The only problem was that, she did not know how to find her bearing in such a dense forest. Nevertheless she decided to go on all the same regardless of what direction she took. She had just started when Toad the Amphibian appeared in front of her and addressed her. 'Little girl, now is your time to escape but you cannot do it on your own. The wizard will soon find that you have escaped and he will follow your trail. He is quite a wonderful athlete. I have watched him run through those bushes like he was wind. I am sure if he gives chase, he will catch up with you in no time. Besides, he could use his flying broom and all sorts of spells.'

'It is you again? What do you want with me this time?'

'I want to help you escape before the wizard comes back', said Toad.

Scared of failing once again, Phoebe was quite willing to give Toad chance. 'Then what are you waiting for. Tell me whatever you want me to do. I promise to do it?' By now tears running down her eyes.

'I am the only one who can take you back to your home.'

Phoebe opened her eyes unable to believe what she had just heard. 'You are the only one who can rescue me? Why, you can't even run faster than me and yet you think you can rescue me', jeered Phoebe.

'Strange isn't it? But that is how things work in this world. Those whom you least expect to do certain things actually do them. I know I am slow on land but I am at an advantage. I hop and do not walk. And because of that it is fairly hard to find my trail', explained the Toad.

'But that is about all you are capable of', protested Phoebe.

'That is what you think but let me tell you that you are in for a surprise', remarked Toad.

Phoebe was getting more impatient; she wanted to get away as quickly as she could. She began to give in 'I want to go back to my home. I want to see my mother', she cried out.

'I know and I am here to help you.'

'Then do it now and stop talking', shouted Phoebe.

'Oh yes I am going to do it. But first I have to explain to you my plan. I am afraid I can only do so by swallowing you up.'

'So that is your rescue plan? Do you think I am that stupid to run away from one man-eater only to allow myself to be eaten by another? Tell me are you one of them wizards?'

'Surely you know toads do not eat humans. Look at my size and compare to yours! I am nothing. Not even the size of your hand. But that does not mean that I can't save you.'

El Pelicano the Pelican stooped to a branch near the ground and called out. 'You are running out of time. Use the spell.'

Phoebe had just about had enough of the talking creatures. She did not have time to question Toad the Amphibian. All she wanted was to get out of the forest and be home. 'Well then, get me out of here. I am no longer concerned with how you do it. Simply go ahead and do it.'

Toad the Amphibian wasted no time. 'Close your eyes', he said. As she did, he uttered the magic words. Almost immediately Phoebe was reduced to the size of an insect. He drew himself closer and swallowed her up. Then he set off hopping through the forest. At one time he found himself on bare ground but he was not scared. He knew no one would hurt him. Just then El Pelicano appeared and grabbed him into its bill and carried him all the way to the river.

The wizard returned home with food both for his captive and himself. He called Phoebe; she was nowhere to be found. He looked round the compound but she was not there. He summoned his magic spells to tell him where Phoebe was but nothing seemed to work. He decided to follow her trail; it did not go so far. 'She must have been carried away by someone. Tell me who it is', the wizard shouted.

'Shouldn't you have listened to your faithful servant the rooster? You knew very well that you were dependent on him and had served you all those years. You were so stupid that you killed him instead. Beauty has brought about your downfall. She has escaped. A toad helped her out', said the genie.

'I will kill that toad if only I knew where it is', cried out the wizard.

'I am afraid you will not. Your days are long gone' answered the genie. Almost immediately lightning struck the man-eating wizard dead.

Meanwhile Toad the Amphibian on his way to Phoebe's home had just crossed the river. It took him another five days to reach Phoebe's home. He got there in the evening when the whole family sat around a huge bonfire as they always did. An old man was telling stories. A little boy saw the toad approaching and rushed to kick it. 'I wouldn't do it if I were you', said the toad.

The little boy scared by what he called a talking toad turned to his brother. 'Have you heard anything?'

'No, I haven't. Unless of course for grandfather with his story.'

He decided to think that there was nothing to worry about. Once again he raised his leg to kick the toad. 'I wouldn't do that. I mean it is up to you. You could easily hurt yourself.'

The little boy called to his brother. 'Bob, this toad speaks.'

'Give me a break. First of all that is called a toad and secondly it does not talk. Just get your act together and kick it off before it jumps into someone's drink', yapped Bob.

'I am scared. May be you can do it', suggested Paddy.

'A good suggestion that one is. Just leave it with the master', commented the toad.

Paddy held his breath and walked away saying, 'I cannot do it. You do it. The creature scared me.'

Bob wasted no time. He took a few steps to gain momentum and swung his leg. His foot landed on the toad, which did not even move. He cried out in agony. 'You little fool! Why did you make me kick a stone?' He sat down to nurse his aching foot.

Toad the Amphibian croaked to clear his voice. 'Young man', he began. 'You did not kick a stone. You kicked me. I am the same little creature who hops about at night hoping to partake of the insects drawn to your bonfire.'

Bob opened his eyes. 'I am sorry, did you just say something.'

'I sure did', replied the toad. 'You kicked me and that is not a nice thing to do.'

'What are you trying to say? Just get lost before I squeeze life out of you', yelled Bob. 'This time I may just throw you into that fire over there.'

'That is a bit cruel but I am not scared. Neither am I going to be bullied by you.'

'Is that a threat?' asked Bob.

'Not as such. Let's call it a friendly warning because next time you might hurt yourself really bad.'

Paddy came in. 'So it talks.'

'Oh, I almost forgot. My name is Toad the Amphibian. I usually come to eat insects but tonight I come to bring your family good news'.

'Go away, stupid creature before I inflict damage on you', yelled Paddy.

'You mean, before you hurt yourself even more.'

'What do you want of me?' Paddy screamed. By now everyone was wondering who he was talking to.

'Well, I don't want you to hurt yourself any more. All I demand is to have a word with Phoebe's parents.' By now the whole household had their attention turned to Toad the Amphibian. 'I am sorry to intrude but I am sure I know something which you do not know', explained the toad. 'I know where Phoebe is.'

Everyone immediately turned attention to the toad. 'Tell us then where she is', demanded Phoebe's father. 'Name your price and we will give you.'

'Well make a nice place for me. Lay down something for her. She is inside me and I am going to spew her out', explained the Toad.

'Are you trying to play with our emotions? How on earth would she get inside you?'

'Why not give me a chance. I am not putting demands on any one. All I want is to give you back your daughter. As you may have suspected, she was indeed captured by the man-eating wizard. At least thank goodness she is still alive.' As the parents began to exchange looks, Toad ordered. 'Now give us room.'

'No disrespect creature, you might think that we are dumb to believe that a whole human being can fit inside the belly of a frog', argued Phoebe's grandfather.

'Well, if you can believe what you see, a toad speaking, couldn't you at least try to believe a little more and do what I say? Do it not for me but for Phoebe.'

'Very well then, we will do just that', said Phoebe's father. 'Should it turn out different, you will have me to deal with.'

'Thank you', said the toad.

They did what he said and sat quietly to watch the toad stretching his muscles to regurgitate Phoebe. He spewed something, which looked like a piece of food that he had on to the ground.

'Is that it?' Phoebe's father asked anxiously. 'You come here to spew what is left of your meal and call that my daughter. What an outrage!'

'Oh yes. That is your daughter alright.'

'That is enough. Simply take back your food and go away', cried Phoebe's mother.

She had hardly completed her statement when Toad the Amphibian uttered his magic words. The whole family watched as the tiny thing that Toad had spewed on the ground began to take shape. It was indeed their daughter lying peacefully in her sleep. She opened her eyes and cried out. 'Where am I? I want my mother.'

'We are all here. Welcome back home.'

The overjoyed father ordered a big celebration to mark the re-union. They listened to her as she told them about the wizard and how the Toad had saved her.

Toad the Amphibian had completed his mission and was ready to go back to where he belonged. He turned to the entire family and said, 'May you always be happy. Remember things are not always what they seem to be. Do not despise someone because of appearance.' With that he he went bouncing into the darkness of the night.

# The Naughty Nosy Girl

# The kitchen flood

Naughty and nosy are not exactly nice words to describe someone but sometimes people do use them. They use them even on the people they love and hold dear at heart. Sometimes it is used out of spite. On other occasions as simply a joke. The Pokrost family were no strangers to these words. The parents used them to describe their children; the children used them to describe each other and once in a while, their parents.

Mr and Mrs Pokrost had two daughters, Heidi and Helma. Heidi was ten but already she was very tall for her age. She was also rather timid. Helma was seven going on to eight but unlike her sister was very outgoing, curiously assertive and very talkative. She was the naughty nosy little girl of the family. In the case of Helma the two words knitted together to form what one could easily mistake to be her other names and goodness me, they seemed to spell out what kind of person she actually was. You can imagine, already at her age, she had lost count of how often she was called naughty or nosy. One would expect some form of resentment, but not with Helma. She seemed to enjoy it so much such that each time she was called so she would beam with smiles of approval.

Well, maybe Helma did not really understand the meaning behind them. Or as the old adage goes, "*Routine waters down Value*", the words had lost their sting. She just did not mind being what people thought she was.

If Helma was born curious, then curiosity had indeed become her trademark. As a baby her searching curiosity was interpreted as an indication of intelligence. Her often deplorable explorations were viewed as characteristic of the makings of a scientist. At first her parents couldn't agree more and they never stopped imagining what a star scholar she would make in the future. However, as time went by questions about the kind of stardom she was heading for started to emerge. She was becoming more like a miniature tornado which though limited to the confines of their house always left a trail of destruction wherever it passed. In fact by the time Helma was a toddler she had just about caused as much havoc as any insane adult would. Like all babies she used her mouth most, eating whatever could be swallowed. Whatever she could not put into her little mouth she ensured that it received at least some damage before being left lying around. For some reason she took pleasure in chewing and destroying books. Newspapers, she would rip apart. If she had a pen or pencil, she would scribble meaningless lines thereby rendering the book unreadable. In the kitchen, she knew what shelves kept what and would help herself to the sugar cubes and some cookies. When she had enough she would throw the rest on the floor.

Mr and Mrs Pokrost loved Helma so much that they never once took offense in her actions. Even their reprimands, if any, were always watered down and passed on with a smile. A typical Mrs Pokrost reprimand ran thus: 'Oh crumps, what have we got here! The little menace has been at it again. You really ought to stop these naughty acts little sister because it is wasteful and above all, it gives your mother too much work to do. Okay little angel. Now go and be a sweetheart. Make sure you don't make the same mess again.'

In a soft subdued and convincing tone Helma would reply in what was already becoming her secret anthem. 'Okay mother and father, I will not do it again.' Yet at the back of her mind some little ideas would already start to form as she planned her next action. True enough she would do something completely different but equally disastrous this time with her defence ready. 'Last time, you told me not to do the same thing again. This time I did something different, is anything the matter?' she would ask with her infectious smile flying everywhere.

Poor parents cornered by crafty interpretation of their messages would simply scratch their heads in humility knowing that little sister had won again. Oftentimes, amidst laughter, they would set about trying to make her understand what they meant. The whole situation would end up being reduced to a laughable incident.

Somehow God had graced Helma with eloquence and ability to critically analyse events albeit for her own good. At five she could reason with adults often times emerging victorious even with her limited vocabulary. She was very persuasive too. Above all she knew when to inject in emotional appeal which always easily melted even the hardest heart of stone. She was a born winner.

Now that the Schools were closed for half-term break, Helma spent most her day with her older sister Heidi under the watchful eye of grandmother who lived in the annex at the back of the main house. As she grew she became more and more curiosity driven. To leave her alone for just five minutes meant a lot of destruction. What is more, she easily twisted the story thereby casting blame on her sister.

Helma enjoyed watching things being done. In fact she never got tired of watching things done in the kitchen. This was partly because she was always able to partake of some food and drink well before the rest of the family. If the food being prepared was bound to take long, she was always given some cookies or cakes to feast on. Sometimes she would help herself to the sugar cubes.

One day, Helma woke up to find that her mother was long gone. She was left all alone with her sister but supposedly under the watchful eye of grandma. 'Where is mother gone?' she demanded of her sister.

'She went to the market and will be back soon. She went to buy for you something special', her sister answered carefully repeating the words mother had told her. 'I am sure you know what that means.' She was trying to excite her sister but Helma showed no reaction. 'We are going to have that special chocolate cake.'

'Is mother going to come back soon?' Helma asked.

'I told you that before'. Heidi knew their mother was not the kind who would walk in and out of the shop without making a tour admiring the goods. 'Of course, mother will soon be here. She cannot afford to be away too long when her favourite girls are at home', answered Heidi.

Helma gave a mischievous smile because she thought she had a brilliant idea. 'I do not want her to come back soon. We have grandma with us.' She edged closer clinging on to her sister arm. 'I want to be with you. I want to play with you. We can do our own things. As long as we do not make lots of noise grandma will not even bother checking.'

Much as she liked the idea Heidi had her reservations. 'You are still a baby. I do not play with babies.'

'Oh no I am a big girl now. I can do things for myself', Helma protested. 'I don't need your help and I am no baby thank you'.

'If that is true why then do you cry a lot? You know what they call children who cry? They call them cry babies', stated Heidi.

'I am not a cry baby. I do not cry because big girls do not cry. Even the song on the television show says that big girls don't cry', Helma affirmed. 'I am a big girl.'

'I don't believe you.' She cocked her head not so much to express her disbelief as to dare her sister to action. 'If what you say is true, what did you do yesterday? You cried just because I went to play with my friends.'

'But that was yesterday. Today I am a big girl. I can even stay at home alone' touted Helma. There was tenderness in her little wicked scheming, just enough to sway anyone to believe her. It was already beginning to work on her sister who by now let her mind wander away a little. She wanted to be with her friends playing but the mere fact that she was left with Helma and grandma who never really seemed to notice anything happening round her except for the books she was always glued on to made it impossible. She thought of taking her along, but dismissed the thought. Helma was always troublesome. She would never give them peace. Besides she would need her mother's permission for both of them to go out. 'May be I could pop out to call my friends', she told herself. 'We can always play here while you Little Sis can do whatever you like over there. Well, not really anything.' She cut shot whatever she wanted to say as what she thought was a brilliant idea flashed through her mind. 'Helma, did you just say that you can stay alone?' she asked.

'Of course I can. I have told you before and I am telling now again, I am a big girl and I can fight for myself. Besides grandmother is at the back of the house pruning the rose plants.' Helma looked at her sister in the face and with a concerned smile asked; 'May I know why you are asking?'

'No. It is not that important.'

'Remember, mother always says we should never lie to one another.' Helma persisted.

'Okay then. It is just because I wanted to go and call Julie to play with us but I just can't leave you in the house alone' Heidi explained. 'Then again we could go together.'

Helma protested. 'Must I really go with you? Julie's house is just round the corner. You can run alone and come back quickly. Even grandma will not notice.'

Heidi was reluctant to leave her sister alone. Not that some bad person would steal her, but for fear of their mother finding that she had left the house without permission. She tried to scare her sister into going with her. 'Little Sis, you know too well that it is not safe to leave you alone. I do not want some nasty people to come and take you away you', said Heidi. 'Of course, I am not going to say anything about ghosts that walk around here'.

'Now I get it. You want to tell me that you are going to stay with Julie for the whole day? In that case we will all go.'

'Oh no, I just wanted to go and call Julie.'

'That is fine. We will all go and leave all the doors open. Did it occur to you that mother never leaves her keys behind? Any way I wouldn't worry, we will be gone for just a few seconds', said Helma.

One thing for certain, Heidi did not want Helma to go with her. She once again asked. 'Are you really big enough to stay at home alone?'

'Yes, I am. I can stay here for up to ten minutes alone while you go for your friend', asserted Helma. 'Just try to get here before mother. As for grandma, she will never know a thing. Okay?'

Heidi asked no more questions. 'I will be back really quickly', she assured her little sister. Then she snuck through the back door and the side gate without arousing grandmother's attention. She ran as fast as she could to call her friend.

'Take your time', Helma said her hands clutching hard upon her doll. She was not scared of being home alone. Well, she did not even think of the dangers involved. All she wanted was to be able to do whatever she wanted without her patronising sister.

No sooner had Heidi disappeared around the corner than Helma abandoned the doll and ran straight to the kitchen. Usually she would go straight for the sugar cubes. This time she wanted to do something that would impress her parents and her sister too. She had watched her mother prepare family dinner every day and she believed she could do the same now. She was going to cook something for the whole family. Just then she found herself asking if she really knew what she wanted to cook and how quickly could it be done. By now she was looking around the kitchen. Her eyes caught sight of the pile of plates from the previous dinner. 'I think I will do the dishes first', she told herself audibly.' Hopefully by the time I finish I will have found what to do.'

Her enthusiasm to do dishes was soon put to the test. She was just a little bit too short to reach the wash basin. She tried to rally all effort but nothing seemed to change the fact that she was short. 'I can do it. I can get to that basin. I can wash those plates', she told herself. The most obvious plan was to jump as high as she could so as to be able to reach the tap across the wash basin for leverage. If she did manage to do that, she could easily sit on the worktop and go about her business. Up she jumped with hands stretched out to catch the tap. Her attempts were thwarted by the fact that mother always turned swivelling tap to face the window thus rendering it out of reach for children. She tried one more time, this time leaning forward as much as she could. She still couldn't reach the tap.

Despite knocking and hitting her chin against worktop she did not give up. Just then she saw a stool around. Her beautiful round eyes shone with delight and her lips gaped into a wide smile. She started to talk to herself rather audibly. 'I said I was going to do it and I am going to do just that. I will climb this stool and I will do what I have to do.' She was soon up on the stool. She put on the water stopper in place inside the wash basin, threw in some wash-up liquid and with a little bit of struggle managed to turn on the tap. She was now at it. Dishes were being washed but she was not standing firmly enough. Her little legs begun to feel pins and needles but she would not give up. Instead she decided to sit besides the wash basin on the worktop. Unfortunately, the stool fell off as she eased herself to sit. Helma opened her eyes wide for there was no way she could come down. Moreover she was the type who did not particularly enjoy jumping from heights. 'I guess I will have to wait here until Heidi comes back', she said out loud. She turned to her work and much to her surprise the sink was now full and water was overflowing on to the floor. 'Oh doodles. What a mess!' She said as she reached out to stop the tap.' She tried but somehow the faucet seemed stuck. She struggled to turn off the water in vain. The tap was too tight for her. 'Oh doodles, now this is what I call trouble. The water is running everywhere in the kitchen and everything is getting soaked. I wish I could do something at least before mother comes back', she cried out. 'Oh, doodles. I just hope grandmother does not come in to see this mess.'

Julie and Heidi arrived to the scene that they did not expect. There was Helma sitting on the worktop. The floor was covered with water and the taps continued to run. Heidi managed to wade through the mini deluge and shut the water. She then put forth the stool for Helma to get down. This was not without complaints. 'Little sister, you have gone way beyond control. This time I will tell mother everything.'

'Go right ahead. Do not forget that it was your fault. You left me alone at home when you should have been here', Helma fought back.

'But I did not tell you to play with the water.'

'I was not playing. I was doing your job. Remember mother always asks you to clean the dishes, did you do them?' She paused to wait for an answer but somehow started to talk again. 'Well sister, I was only trying to help you.'

Helma's threat softened Heidi's attack. She realised that arguing was doing them no good. They had to get rid of the water before their mother's return. She called out to her sister. 'Stop that yapping and get down to work. We ought to get this place clean before mother comes back.'

'You forgot Grandma. Do I need to remind you that she will soon be coming for her mid-morning tea?' yapped Helma.

'Don't worry she is too busy enjoying the morning sun to notice what is happening. Just come and start working', commanded Heidi.

'How are you going to do that? There is water everywhere.' Helma commented.

'We will scoop it with a cup and throw it into the sink.'

They were about to do that when they realised that the basin stopper was sitting tight under the plates and there was no way they could take it off. 'Well, Little Sis, you did your job properly. Now we can't even use the sink. I suppose the best we can do is to throw the water through the window.'

'Why not pour it through the back door?' Julie asked.

'Well, grandma might pick interest in the action. I swear you don't want her involved. She can shout and even spank. We may well have to settle for the window.'

'I have an idea', jumped Helma. 'Yes, the vacuum cleaner! We are going to use the vacuum cleaner to suck out the water.' She was all smiles. 'I told you I would come up with the best solution.'

'But I have never seen mum use it to mop up water' remarked Heidi.

Helma was on the roll and nothing was going to stop her. 'Girl, listen to me. Trust me on this. If vacuums can suck dust what stops them from sucking water?' she argued. By now she had made up her mind. She was not going to wait for any more suggestion. She grabbed the vacuum cleaner, plugged it into the socket and let the go the power switch. The suction noise seemed to suggest it was working. Then suddenly there was a loud bang as the machine flew into the air. Almost immediately there was a black out.

'My clever Little Sis! Always full of bright ideas. What next? Now the power is gone too, what are we going to do?' Heidi commented with blatant sarcasm.

'Never mind, father will fix the lights when he comes back. As for now we have to go on working. We have to throw the water through the window', replied Helma in a rather commanding voice. 'I will sit here on the work top. You and Julie will pass the water for me to throw through the window.'

Without word they lined up to work. Helma sat on the counter by the window. She was charged with throwing the water out of the window. Heidi and Julie meanwhile did the scooping.

Tommy had followed his sister Julie. He did not want to be seen so he had hidden at the back of the house by the kitchen window waiting for an opportunity to be invited to join the play. When he could not hear the girls talking, he decided to elevate himself on the garden stool to take a peek through the open window. The sight of water on the floor surprised him. He was so shocked that he simply stood there with an open mouth. Unfortunately, it was a wrong time and a wrong place to keep the mouth open. For Helma was just throwing the first pan of water through the window. It caught Tommy on the face. He screamed, 'Ouch! That water went right into my mouth.'

Helma had the right words for him. 'What on earth were you doing there with an open mouth? You know you shouldn't have been there in the first place. Secondly, I have a job to do and I will continue throwing water on you unless you get away from there.' She let go another pan of water.

'Ouch! Stop it, you are making me wet.'

'Did I hear somebody like Tommy calling from outside?' asked Julie.

'May be but I surely do not see anyone.' She raised the tone of her voice. Well, you know what that means. I have to continue working for mother must find the place dry.'

By now Tommy was crying out loud. 'You have spoiled all my clothes with dirty water. I am going to tell my mother. I am not your friend anymore.'

The entire team had to abandon the work temporarily. Heidi and Julie knew at once that they had to stop Tommy from blowing their secret. They hurried outside and were soon standing side by side with water drenched Tommy. Although the situation called for laughter they had to content themselves with muffled giggles while at the same time trying to make peace with him.

Julie meanwhile talked to her brother in a more conciliatory manner. 'Tommy, we are sorry for this mess. We will dry your face and then you and I will run home to get you changed. By the way you can have some of my sweets too.'

Tommy beamed with smile. 'Really, I can take any amount I want?'

'Oh yes. You can take half and leave the other half for me.'

'Thanks Julie. You are the best sister ever and I love you.'

'That is okay. Let us say anything for the nicest boy in the world.'

'You really mean that, do you?' Tommy asked.

Heidi cut in with a perfect sweet lie. 'We were just talking before we discovered that you were hiding around. You know we are tired of leaving you behind. We want you to be in our play group.' She tapped his nose fondly. 'What do you think about that?'

'Thanks, I would love to be one with you', answered Tommy in between sobs.

Heidi wasted no time. She immediately injected in conditions. 'However, we will only allow you in on one condition. That you tell no one what happened.'

'But she threw dirty water on me. She is not my friend', mumbled Tommy. 'That, I must surely report to Auntie Pokrost. We don't want her get away with throwing dirty water on people, do we?'

'Well, that was just a mistake. She never intended it. I am sure we can forget it this one time. Now we will find a way of drying your clothes.'

They managed to make peace with Tommy, but it was short lived. Mrs Pokrost came back from her shopping and found them standing outside. Her eyes caught on Tommy in wet and dirty attire. 'What In the name of happy angels happened to you Tommy?'

'Nothing auntie Pokrost', he rubbed his eyes 'Really nothing.'

'Then that nothing must have been … well, I don't know. Look at you!'

'Auntie, I was playing in.... pla...y...' Tommy stammered.

'Tommy, I am waiting', Mrs Pokrost said her eyes fixed sternly on the little boy.

'I was playing in the garden and I fell down. Yes, in the garden near the pond.' Tommy was trying his best to avoid the question. 'Any way auntie, I must be gone to change from these dirty clothes.'

She called out in her deep scary voice. 'And where do you think you are going?' She grabbed Tommy's hand and led him to the front room. She left Tommy standing on the door mat as she grabbed hold of a towel to wipe his face. 'Now we will go through it one more time. Cut out all the lies. Tell me the truth and only the truth.' Her action set the little boy shaking. She noticed it but continued her line of questioning. 'Tommy what happened to you? Do not let me beat it out of you. You know and I know too that it has not rained for a good while now.' Mrs Pokrost had her own ways of getting the truth. She knew immediately that something was wrong. 'Tommy if something was wrong you would tell me, wouldn't you? I mean I do not have to remind you how God deals with children who tell lies.'

Tommy sighed. He counted the number of little lies he had said since the previous day and they were quite many. 'I will tell God that I am sorry. I have told ten lies already.'

'Well, why don't you come with me to the kitchen? I have something in these bags for you.'

Tommy stayed on door mat by the front door. As for the girls, they had already disappeared into hiding. She opened the passage way door leading to the kitchen. All her attention was focused on Tommy at the main door. As she took another step into the kitchen she slipped and fell face down scattering the shopping she had just brought home. She was soaked to the bone. Tommy heard the fall and rushed to the scene. 'I am sorry Mrs Pokrost.'

She was simply not listening. She called out loud 'Heidi, I want you here right now. I want you to tell me who made this mess.'

'It looks like a swimming pool', remarked Tommy.

Mrs Pokrost response to Tommy's remark was quite humorous. 'Well, big enough for a few frogs to swim in', she said. 'And I take it this is the pond you were referring to.'

Heidi came trembling. She saw her mother dripping wet. 'Sorry mother.'

'I am sure you will truly be sorry when I am finished with you. Now, first things first: who did this?'

'Not me.'

'I suppose you are going to tell me who 'Not Me' is or else I am going to give you a hiding to remember. Do I make myself clear?'

Her message was received. 'Mother, it was Little Sis.' Heidi answered in a trembling voice. She knew there was going to be a lot of trouble. Mrs Pokrost was not easy to convince.

'I am going to ask you one more time. Who created this mess?'

'Mother, it wasn't me. It was Little Sis.' Tears poured down her eyes. 'I did not do it. Little Sis left the tap running.'

Mrs Pokrost was convinced that it was Heidi who did it. In her mind Helma was too young to do such. She bellowed on. 'I am tired of this talk. Everything is Little Sis. Tell me how on earth could she reach the tap? How could she lift all those plates?' She grabbed hold of Heidi and threatened to smack her little buttocks with a sandal. 'When I leave you in charge, I do not expect you to mess up my home', she said.

Julie came out from where she was hiding. She looked at her friend. She was screaming. Mrs Pokrost had one of her sandals in the hand raised ready to smack Heidi. Julie tried to arouse her attention but Mrs Pokrost was concentrating. 'I must do something to help my friend', Julie told herself. Without word she ran and with her little hands grabbed hold of Mrs Pokrost's sandal making it hard for her to swing it.

'Who do you think you are? When my children misbehave I discipline them', roared Mrs Pokrost. 'Now if you will, please leave now.'

Julie did not move. She started to talk in defence of her friend. 'Auntie Pokrost, my mother disciplines me too when I do wrong. She has never done so when I am right.' Somehow she had managed to get Mrs Pokrost's attention.

'Talk I am listening', roared Mrs Pokrost. 'You have already stopped me from teaching this worthless child what it means to be responsible.'

'Auntie, you came home and found the water in the kitchen. You straight away thought it was Heidi and was ready to punish her for it.'

'Young lady, I know my daughters. Who else could do such a thing but Heidi here?'

'It was not Heidi because I was with her all the time. That mess was created by Little Sis. She used a stool to reach the wash basin. Ask her?'

Mrs Pokrost dropped the sandal. She felt embarrassed and apologised to Heidi. Just then Helma emerged from where she was hiding laughing. 'That was quite a spanking you gave Heidi. There is one problem however.' She began to giggle. 'Do you know that poor girl had nothing to do with the water in the kitchen?'

'Wait a minute. What are you trying to say?'

'You heard me. It wasn't Heidi. It was me.' Suddenly she started to cry. 'I did not really mean to do it though. I guess I wanted to impress you. Unfortunately things went wrong. I am truly sorry. I am sorry you had to beat my sister for no fault of hers.' Helma was never short of tears. They poured down in such torrents that even Mrs Pokrost's anger melted away. She threw the sandal away and became more apologetic. 'I am sorry girls.' She kissed Heidi and went on to reassure her. 'I am sorry. I want you and indeed everyone here to know this; no matter what, a mother will always love her children. When out of anger she smacks you, it does not mean the end or that she hates you. On the contrary she does it out of love. Put it this way, she is simply trying to teach you that love is not always about being sweet. Love is also about pointing and putting one on the right way. When I discipline you girls, it is because I want you to grow well and be responsible people.'

There was silence as Mrs Pokrost explained herself. Even those who had been crying dried their tears and listened to each and every word she said. 'I have an idea. May be we can all clean up this mess. As we do it I will tell you a story. It has to do with kitchen floods like this one.'

Mrs Pokrost and the girls set about to clear the water. As they worked she told her story. 'My story is about some naughty boys who ruined their neighbour's house. Like all good lads, they started with good intentions. They wanted to wash the floor. They let the water flow, putting in some soap and started to scrub it. One of them accidentally fell down on his backside and because of the soapy water slid across the room. His friends thought it was funny. They also started to skate on their behinds.'

'What happened next, Mrs Pokrost?' inquired Tommy.

'They enjoyed the game so much that they forgot they were supposed to clean the house. And what more, they forgot water running.'

'You mean just like Helma did today', continued Tommy.

'Yes but it was a lot more than that. The water flowed into the neighbour's house. Now the neighbouring house had the most expensive carpet in the area. Apparently that carpet was a gift from the king. In the entire country only two homes had them, the king's and that house.'

Tommy wanted to ask another question but Mrs Pokrost signalled to him to wait. 'The king had instructed the man never to let water touch the carpet for if it did, nobody would ever visit his house again.' By now the water was all cleared and everything was in its place. The children stood on waiting for Mrs Pokrost to complete the story. Instead she changed the topic. 'Now I will fix some tea for all of us. I have some cookies too.'

'But mother what happened to the boys and to the neighbour?' Heidi asked.

'Nobody ever visited him again. As for the boys, they were punished for doing it.'

'Oh no, you mean the poor man never got any visitors at all?' insisted Heidi. 'Didn't he have friends?'

'Of course he had friends.'

'But why didn't they visit him?' asked Julie.

'Well, the reason is pretty obvious. The smell of a wet carpet can really be offensive to the nose.'

'I am sure the man could have had it dried', Tommy commented.

'He did. He even employed the best cleaner and used the most expensive odour removers but the smell overpowered them all.'

The children once again burst into laughter. As for Mrs Pokrost the time had come to drive home her message. 'Well children, there is a lot that we can learn from that. First of all, be careful! Never let your good intentions inflict disaster on others.'

Helma opened her big round eyes and said out aloud, 'I am sorry for all I did. I am sorry Heidi was spanked because of my fault. I will never do it again.'

Mrs Pokrost made no comment about the incident again. Instead she went on to invite the children to tea. 'Now we shall have our tea.' She turned to Tommy. 'I suppose you will need to change those wet clothes before we sit down. You could always wear Helma's T-shirt and shorts.'

'Thanks auntie Pokrost but there is no way I am going to wear girl's clothes,' Tommy remarked. By now the girls were all giggling. 'I guess you can see my point. They are already laughing before I even put them on.' He looked at Mrs

Pokrost. 'I will be right back'. He ran through the door to their home.

With Tommy gone attention was drawn to the tea. 'Auntie Pokrost, I am not sure we can make the tea', Julie remarked.

'Is there anything else that I ought to know?' Mrs Pokrost enquired.

Helma did not wait to talk. 'Mother, I am sorry about the vacuum cleaner too', she started. 'I thought we could use it to suck out the water. Well, it worked for a few seconds then it made noise and the lights went out. As you can see nothing seems to be working. Even the refrigerator stopped.'

'You are saying the electric is cut out as well?'

'I think so. Nothing seems to be working', explained Heidi.

'That should not stop us from having our tea. I will try to fix it. If I fail then we will have to wait. Your father will look into that when he comes. In the meantime I hope everyone has learnt a lesson from this. Now you will all have your tea. I always keep hot water in a flask. So we can still have our tea.'

As the girls settled down for tea, Heidi remembered her grandmother. 'Are we forgetting grandma? Should I call her?'

'I don't think so. The old girl knows the right time to catch up with the rest of the family. She can smell food from miles and miles away.' The old lady commented as she announced her arrival. She brought with her some carrot cake. 'I thought we could use some of this with our tea', she added.

Mrs Pokrost disappeared under the cellar with her torch looking for the main switchboard. 'It is just as I thought', she told herself as she flicked the mains switch back on. She returned to join the rest of the team. 'Now you can have as much tea as you want because I have sorted the electric problem as well.'

Tommy too returned to tea. The first few minutes were spent in silence as everyone savoured grandmother's delicious carrot cake. Helma had some burning questions that had to be asked. 'Mother, what lessons did you learn from the flood incident?'

'A lot but the most important one is that never react until you got your facts right.' She put down her tea on to the saucer. 'When I got in I just reacted. If I had had my facts right then I would have been acting. You reacted to the plates in the sink but did not think of what could happen. That is why we ended up in the flood mess. So, always think before you act. We don't always have control over our reactions but we can control our actions.'

'What are you on about? Am I missing anything?' Grandma Nellore asked.

'We had a minor internal deluge caused by, guess who. It has all been sorted. All is well now. Let us do what we are here for. Do not let the tea get cold', Mrs Pokrost explained. She brushed aside another of Helma's incidents as she always.

# Helma Wanders into the streets

Helma never went to the same school with her sister Heidi. Every morning they set out on their different journeys. Heidi went on the school bus. As for Helma she did not need transport. Her mother used to walk her to and from school. Although the school was near where they lived, they never followed the main roads. Mrs Pokrost believed in shortcuts. She would walk through the back alleys with her daughter's book bag in one hand and the other holding Helma. Every school day Helma religiously followed her mother through the alleys on the way to school and on the way back home. With time Helma became very convinced that she could find her way to school and home alone. She expressed her intention to her mother who simply reminded her to wait until she was old enough. She knew what that meant. Even when for some reason her mother was late to pick her up from school, she would wait for her.

One day the Mrs Pokrost was really very late to pick her up. Helma sat on a pew watching children her age walking on the streets alone. They are no bigger than me and they can be left to roam the streets alone, she told herself. One of these days I will ask mother to let me come to school alone. I know she will love it and she will be proud of me. Suddenly she began to smile and to talk to herself. 'May be mother expects me to find my way home. May be today is my day to show her that I can take care of myself. Yes, I can do it. I can walk home.' She stood up and found herself repeating the Highway Code for crossing the roads:

*'Stop! Look Left then Right, and then Left again. If it is clear cross the road.*
*Always walk on the pedestrian walkways.*
*At the lights wait for the lights to turn red and for the green man to appear before you cross.*
*Always use the Zebra crossing.'*

She felt she knew a lot and was ready to go. She looked around for her teacher. She was quite busy with her work. The other child who had been waiting with her was being collected by her mother. Now is my time to go, Helma told herself. She plucked up courage and went to her teacher. 'Miss Charity, I am not sure if my mother is going to come.'

'Do not worry I can always wait with you', Miss Charity said.

'Of course you will. I just thought maybe I could join Rachel and her mother. They live quite near us. I mean Rachel's mother can always walk me home. If my mother is not there, I can always play with Rachel until she comes back. And of course if mother came here, you would tell her where I am, wouldn't you.'

Miss Charity sat there speechless. Lots of questions went through her mind. For all she knew, she was a teacher charged with responsibility to look after children until their parents picked them up. There were times when some of them were picked by neighbours. She recalled a particular incident when Mrs Pokrost actually walked Rachel to their home.

'You do not have to let me go. I mean I can always wait whatever length of time until my mother comes. I only thought it would make things a little easy for you. I mean if you do not have something else to do, it is okay with me. I will wait right here', Helma reasoned.

In no time Miss Charity was convinced. She needed time to prepare her lessons for the next day. 'I suppose I can tell your mother that you went with Rachel's mother. Now off you go.'

Helma did not wait to hear anymore word. She grabbed her bag and ran as fast as she could. She managed to cross the road safely, but could not see Rachel and her mother anywhere. She stopped a little and asked herself which way to follow. 'My mother usually follows that way', she said her finger pointing at the alley way. 'I think for a change I will follow the main road. She walked on from time to time singing. Then she came to the shopping centre and found her eyes glued on to the rolling demo of toys. 'Wow, that one is cute. I will tell mother to buy me one.' Just then she saw an even prettier one. 'Oh wow! That is the real one I want. I must go in and ask the price.'

She walked in and was immediately met by a shop assistant. Helma never waited to be asked, she always did it first. 'Excuse me Miss. Those toys in the window! How much do they cost?'

'Little lady, they cost quite a penny. Lots of .....'

Helma broke in. 'Then I can have two of them for myself and the other for my sister. You see Miss, I have been saving my pennies and I do not mind spending them on toys.' She put down her books and pulled out two coppers. 'Here you go. I want one toy for my sister and one for me. Come! I will show you which ones I like.' She held the shop assistants skirt and started to lead her to the window.'

'Wait a minute little lady! Your two pennies are good but unfortunately they cannot buy that toy. I mean they cannot buy anything.'

'Why? Didn't you just say that they cost a penny?' queried Helma.

'I did not exactly say they cost one penny each did I? I am sorry but you need a lot more than what you have.'

'How much more do I need?' Helma asked.

'Several thousands of pennies, is what you will need.'

'Well I do not know what a thousand pennies look like but I will try to save that amount. Meanwhile can I have back my money, please?' She held out her hand with a smile on her face.

'Here you go young lady. May be we see you next time when you have saved up enough.'

'You left out one possibility?'

'And what may that be little lady?'

'You may not be seeing me another time.' She smiled and started to walk towards the door but turned back towards the assistant. 'I am sorry but there is just one thing I should like to make clear. I do not mean to offend anyone but is that the way you treat all your customers?'

The shop assistant opened her eyes unable to figure out where she had gone wrong. If anything she was beginning to detest the girl before her. She declined to answer.

'Any way, take it from me. Every customer likes to be told the cost of things in clear terms. And for your information they walk in here because they actually see what they want. Do not just think of me. I mean I really wanted the doll but it is beyond my budget.' She smiled briefly. 'Like I said, always tell your customer the price in simple, positive and friendly terms. Never tell them that they cannot afford it. That is all I have to say.'

Helma turned to walk out only to hear someone clap in applause. 'Young lady, please come back here', the young man who was applauding called at Helma. 'I promise I will pay for the items you wanted.'

'I would love that but mother always says never accept free gifts from people you do not know. Thanks any way. I really have to go home now.' She started to walk towards the door.

Helma's comment made the poor shop assistant feel guilty for there was plenty of truth in it. 'Little sister', she called at Helma who was by now approaching the main door. 'Has anyone ever told you that you have a big mouth?'

Helma stopped then turned around to answer the question. 'You have now.' Her comment made the lady shop assistant want to disappear. 'Any way Miss, you didn't need to. I know that my mouth is big. I found it out when I managed to put a full dough nut in it.' She stood there grinning as on lookers rolled with laughter. 'You may want to know that I can even put a full banana into my mouth. Good day miss, I have to really go now.' She walked out leaving everyone laughing.

'She may indeed have a big mouth but she is also intelligent. I think if you put in practice what she has said you will be the best salesperson in this shop. I only wish we could see her more often', the supervisor remarked. He called the shop assistant away from the customers. 'I heard everything that child said and I think it is true. I suppose you will be put that into practice.'

'I am sorry, sir.'

'Any way, which toy was she interested in?'

'One of those in the display window,' replied the shop assistant.

'See to it that she gets one, courtesy of me. She has been brilliant in training us.'

'But she has already gone. I don't suppose you want me to start running after her?'

'No, I want you to gift wrap one of them and have it sent to her school. Her school uniform tells us where to send it. And I do suppose you bothered to read her name badge.'

'Sorry, I did not.'

'Helma Pokrost is her name. See to it that she gets that present, will you?'

Helma had walked for almost five minutes when she came by an ice cream man. She stopped and took out her coins. May be I can use them for an ice cream, she told herself. She decided to ask for the price. 'Excuse me mister! Can you tell me if my money is enough for an ice cream cone, please?'

The ice cream man looked at the two pennies and smiled. 'I am afraid not. You need a lot more than that. You need at least 100 pennies. That means you still need another 98 pennies.'

'That sounds a lot but I suppose I have to go on saving until one day I can walk in and take my pick.' She put away her money. 'By the way, when you were little did you also have to save money for ice cream?'

'Not particularly', replied the ice-cream man.

'How then did you manage to have all this ice cream?'

'Little Sister, I had to work for it. I use to go about telling jokes and being paid for it. You know, there are people out there who would give anything for a really good joke.'

'But making people laugh is not difficult. I can make you laugh right now.'

'Do not even waste your time. Nobody ever makes me laugh.'

'What will you give me if I make you laugh?'

'Let us say, an ice lolly.'

'Well Mister, you are on. You have just got yourself a deal. Be prepared for laughter, for standing in front of you is the funniest kid in the block.' She stood there staring at nothing in particular but with a little innocent smile. She started to talk. 'This morning I made my teacher laugh. I told her about the famous saying.'

'What is that?'

'Nothing really special. I suppose I could tell you as well. Who knows it might make you also laugh. It is about the old saying that *'Two heads are better than one'*.

'Little Sister, that is true. As you grow up, you will find out more about it. It is true and will always be true.'

A few more people walked in much to Helma's delight. She took a deep breath. 'I do not know what to say. If you accept the saying, then you will also accept it that two idiots are better than one wise person. Or for that case two monkeys are better than one Ice cream man.'

The ice cream man burst into laughter. 'I cannot imagine two monkeys being better than one human being.'

'Sorry mister, did I just hear you laugh? I guess you know what that means?'

'Monkeys are animals.' The ice-cream man continued to laugh. 'I can never imagine in a million years, two monkeys being better than one ice cream man? You are really having a laugh aren't you?'

'Sir, you are the one laughing, not me', she commented much to the onlookers delight. 'The question here is about heads. Nobody actually stated what kind of heads. In any case, the deal was to make you laugh which I have done.'

Helma went on telling the few jokes and riddles she knew. The ice cream man laughed and laughed. He stopped to serve a customer. Helma too said nothing. When the customer left she turned on her jokes again. 'Do you know what a small mother is called?'

'I suppose little mother'

'Wrong. She is called minimum. You know the opposite of maximum.'

'You are good. You have a good sense of humour. Who knows may be one day you will turn out to be the greatest comedian in the world.'

'Leave the future alone. May I remind you that I have won the bet? May I have my ice lolly please?'

The man had been so impressed by her jokes that he actually allowed Helma to choose whatever she wanted. She took a vanilla flavoured ice cream cone. She stood erect, smiled at the man. Then she stretched out her little hand to his. 'Thank you for the ice cream. It has been nice doing business with you.' She headed down the street.

She kept walking and from time to time stopping to admire the shop displays. Ideas started to flow through her head. She thought of her mother. She pictured her going to school and being told that I had already left. She would go and check with Rachel's mother. 'Oh pickles! How is she going to react when she finds that I am not there? She is going to scream at the teacher and everybody else', she told herself. She turned on to the street and headed straight to the house which she thought was theirs. 'I am sure mother will be surprised to see me arrive on my own. But knowing my mother, she will probably smack me first. Anyway, I will have to wait.' She rung the bell and waited for someone to open the door. Just then she heard a dog barking from inside. She wanted to run away but then the door opened. An old man came out to meet her.

'What can I do for you', he asked.

'Well sir, I am really sorry I must have got the wrong house. May be I am actually on the wrong street. Then again, it is not really my fault all these streets look the same to me. Anyway Sir, I am sorry it is a wrong door. Good day sir.'

She did not wait for the old man to answer back. She simply retraced her steps fast. Half way down the street she started to talk to herself again. 'I am beginning to think that I am really lost.' She tried the next street. This time she not only heard one dog but several. She did not wait for anyone to open the door. 'That is it. I am lost but I must find my way home.' She adjusted her bag. 'How am I supposed to get home? I think I will just go back to school and wait for the teachers to call my mother.' She crossed her hands over her chest. 'There is just one problem. I am not sure I know which way goes to school.' She was engaging herself in a monologue. 'I think I will just continue walking until I meet somebody I know then I will ask for the way home or to school.'

Helma had been walking for almost two hours and her little feet were beginning to ache. She wanted to sit but the streets were not all that clean. 'I will walk back to the shopping centre. I know there are a few benches that I can sit on' she told herself. But with the fatigue encroaching, her paces were becoming slower and slower. She managed to reach the shops and was about to sit when she saw a policeman on patrol. 'I think I have found my way home. That policeman will take me home. If he cannot then at least he will bring me to school' she muttered. She went straight to the policeman. 'Hello Mr. Policeman, I wonder if you have a minute to spare. I have some important questions that must be answered.'

'All right young lady. Let's say I answer your questions after which you answer mine as well.'

'You got yourself a deal', Helma replied stretching out her hand to the policeman. She hesitated a little before firing her questions. 'Mr. Policeman, what would you do if you got really lost and could not find your way home?'

'Let us see. I think I will seek help. I will ask the first person I see. If I was lucky to find a policeman then I would ask him. You see policemen know all the streets' the policeman explained.

'What about if you are lost simply because you do not know the name of the street you are looking for? Say you have been to that address before but for some reason forgot the street name.'

'Then you certainly must remember the name of the person you are going to see. You can use their name to find them.'

'You have answered all my questions. Now I want to tell you that I am lost. I left school thinking that I could find my way home all by myself but I have failed. I am sure my mother is busy looking for me. If only I could find my way to school I am sure I could get back home.' Big balls of tears were beginning to form in her eyes.

'My dear lady don't you worry. I will make sure that you get back to your mother in one piece. Now, if you do not mind, it is my turn to ask you some questions.'

'Go on then. I am ready' said Helma with a little smile.

'Wow, did you know that you look beautiful when you smile with tears in your eyes? Any way question one. What is your name?'

'Helma Pokrost. And before you say anything else, it is Pokrost. It is spelt as in roast pig meat but without the first "R" and without letter "A". She sounded it. 'Remember "ROST" as in "FROST". That is my family name. But everybody likes to call me Naughty Nosy Girl and I like it.'

'Okay, I will also call you Naughty Nosy Girl. Do you know what your mother's name?'

'She is Mrs Gilda Pokrost and my father is called Mr Dean Pokrost. I do not know if they have other names. Oh yes, my father is a bus driver.'

'This will do. Now just one more question. What school do you go to?'

'I have never bothered to know but I think it is written on my book bag somewhere.' Helma took the bag off her back. 'Oh yes my home is not far from the Heroes Memorial stone. If I get to that stone I can find my way home. All the people on that street know my father because he is a bus driver.'

'Little madam, say no more. Thank you so much. You can now relax because you are not so far from home. I will take you there myself.

'Thanks ever so much.'

'No worries. It is my job and besides it is the least one can do for an old friend's daughter. You see, your father and I went to the same school when we were kids.'

'If that is the case can I call you Uncle Policeman?'

'If you like, but I would rather you use my real names because it sounds better. Sam Frogg is the name.' Helma opened her eyes because she felt the name was strange. Just then the policeman interrupted. 'I should like to set the record right before you start getting wrong ideas. My name is spelt with two g's not one. In other words, it has nothing to do with the little animal called frog.'

'Don't you worry, because if you don't want to be called uncle policeman then I choose to call you Uncle Sam.'

Meanwhile Mrs Pokrost was running from house to house asking for her daughter. She had been assured by Rachel's mother that she had not come with them. She phoned Miss Charity and gave her piece of mind. She had waited long enough and decided to phone the police. Just as she put down the phone the doorbell rang. She rushed to open it and there was her daughter with a police officer. She grabbed her into her arms. 'Oh my sweet dumpling why did you leave before mother arrived? You had me worried to the bones. You know mother loves you so much.'

'I love you too and I am sorry. I only thought I was going to save you a journey to school. I was wrong. I got lost. But uncle Frogg found me.'

'You found Uncle Frogg, you mean?'

'Yes, I found uncle and he was able to help.

Mrs Pokrost looked at the man in uniform. 'This is wonderful. Step right in. How did you bump into this naughty girl?'

'I must say she came to me when she found that she was lost. And would you believe that she was actually near hear? She was just one block away.'

The ice cream man drove by and stopped his van not far from the Pokrost house. He saw Helma and called out, 'how is my little comedian friend?'

Helma waved back. 'I am very well, thank you. This is where I live', she added. By now she was edging towards the van.

'Any more jokes for the poor ice-cream man?'

'I have run out of jokes for today. If however, you are in such a good mood then perhaps I could have two ice cream cones, one for my sister and the other for me.'

'For a friend like you, anything', the man said as he handed Helma her favourite ice cream flavour.

Helma was about to walk away when her mother arrived. 'How much do I owe you for the two ice creams?'

'It has all been taken care of. They are on the house.' As Mrs Pokrost stood there counting her luck, the man went on to explain the offer. 'Earlier on, I met your daughter on the streets. I must say she is one good comedian. She promised to make me laugh in exchange for ice cream. And she did just that. She is one wonderful child I must say. You are a lucky woman to have such a wonderful daughter. Guide her properly. There are a few of the kind in the world.'

The words touched Mrs Pokrost so much that she kept to herself all the words she had planned to say. 'Thank you, for the lovely comment. I will cherish them', she said.

That night Mrs Pokrost had a private audience with her two girls during which she reminded them the need to obey what they are told. The two girls promised their mother to always obey what their parents said. Helma was reminded to apologise to her teachers.

Early the next morning Mrs Pokrost woke up her daughters and set about preparing them for school. Heidi as usual had her lunch packed. Off she went to wait for her bus. When she was ready Helma walked with her mother to school. This time, they set off a little bit earlier than normal. This was because Mrs. Pokrost needed to apologise to Miss Charity.

# A visit to the farm

Mrs Pokrost had a sister in the countryside. The Pokrosts had been invited to spend a few days with the Hogg family on their farm. This was going to be the first time for Heidi and Helma to visit their auntie Hogg. They had heard lots about her and the wonderful farm they had and were looking forward to it.

They packed their belongings ready for the holiday of a life time. Wellington boots for trekking round the farm, swimming costumes just in case they had to jump into the private lake they had heard so much about and track suits and jeans. Gifts for Uncle and Auntie Hogg were wrapped and packed away safely ready for the trip. Helma wished she had gifts the animals. 'Mother, what do you think I should buy for the cows, pigs and the chickens?' she asked. 'It is very unfair of us to go empty handed to them.'

'What did you have in mind, a bale of hay?'

'They eat that every single day. I want something really special for each one of them. T-shirts, may be?'

'Little woman, farm animals do not really care about the things we humans fret about. As long as they are healthy and have their food, they are happy.'

'So what do you suggest we buy?'

'Nothing, but I have an idea', she said with her index finger pointing across her face. She watched her daughter's face brighten as excitement continued to brew. 'You could always help round the farm when we get there. I am sure Uncle Hogg could use an extra hand to feed the animals.'

'You mean I could actually put food in my hands and let the animals lick it?'

Mrs Pokrost nodded. 'Oh yes, you can allow them, especially the little ones with their rough tickly tongues to lick your hand. But do not try it with the pigs.'

'The pigs too are animals aren't they?'

'They sure are but they may just mistake your fingers for food. If you do not want to lose your fingers, leave the pigs alone.'

'Okay mother. We shall not feed the pigs, just the cows and the chickens.'

And so it was that Mr and Mrs Pokrost and the girls set off to visit the Hoggs. As they meandered away from the maze of urban streets to the narrow winding country roads, Heidi buried herself in the book about heroic ghost busters. She couldn't care less about what was going on. As for Helma her mind was focused on what was to come. The farm was the most fascinating place Helma had ever visited. At least in as far as animals and play were concerned. Until this day she had only known about cows, pigs and hens through pictures and as food. She had never really seen a living one. This was her chance.

They arrived just when cows were being milked. For once in her life Helma stood and watched quietly as the man pulled the teats of the cow carefully directing milk into the pail. She could not understand why the cow did not run away. She moved closer and cautiously touched the cow. At first it did not respond. When she did it again, the cow swung the tail and hit her gently on the face. She did not cry. Instead she moved closer and decided to squat closer by the man milking cows. Like all children of her age, she started to ask lots of questions. 'What are you doing?' she asked.

'Milking cows', the herdsman replied. 'Getting milk from the cow, that is what I am doing.'

'Why are you doing it?'

'Because that is how you get milk from the cow. Put it this way, you get milk by pulling the cow's teats.'

'We get milk from the supermarkets in big bottles', Helma stated.

'That is well said but did you know that all the milk they sell in supermarkets comes from farm animals?'

'I heard about it but did not know how they extracted it.' She looked at the cow. It didn't seem to mind. She was just munching away the hay. 'Doesn't it hurt the cow?'

'Not really. We do it gently. Do you want to try? Here come!'

Helma did not wait. Straight away she joined him. 'What do I do?' she asked.

'Press the teat to squeeze out the milk. Do it like this', the man demonstrated.

Helma tried but no milk came. 'Squeeze it gently', repeated the man.

She did and a drop of milk fell in the pail. She was getting excited. 'I can do it', said Helma. She tried it again. This time a lot more milk came out. 'Wow that is a lot of milk.'

She was beginning to enjoy it when the herdsman interrupted. 'Right, young lady, you have had your go, we do it again tomorrow. I have a few more to go and I am running out of time.'

She moved just a few feet away and started to ask her questions once again. 'Where does the milk come from?'

'You see that sack-like pouch underneath the cow? I am talking about the one on which the teats are attached. It is called an udder. Inside it you find milk.'

'How does it get there?' Helma fired another question.

Nobody had ever asked him such a question. Even if it had been asked, he did not really know the answer. Nevertheless he went on to give his view. 'It is a long story but let's say it is from the food they eat. Cows process their food in a special way so as to produce milk for their calves.'

'You mean to say milk comes from grass? I mean that is the only food that cows eat.'

'In a way but the grass gets processed inside the cow.'

'But when I was a small baby I used to suck my mother's breast. Milk came out of it as well. Was it because my mother ate grass too?'

The question was hard to explain. Moreover, he had had only a little education. He knew the time had come to avoid the question. 'My dear friend', he said trying to avoid the question. 'Sorry, what did you say your name was?'

'I did not tell you my name but if you want call me Little Sis. And you, what are you called?'

'I am Hardy the herdsman. I grew up on the farm. I enjoy looking after animals. Any way, you asked me a really difficult question. Quite honestly I have never thought of the answer. All I know is that if the cows are well fed and given enough water they produce lots of milk. Perhaps you could reserve your question for your teachers at school.'

Helma did not say a thing. She stood there fascinated by the way Hardy was milking the cows. One after another he milked them. She finally broke her concentration and begun once again to ask questions. 'I am just thinking maybe I should leave school and become a herds girl.'

'May be you ought to finish school first. I mean learn a lot about animals and then come out here to help them. Your cousin, Master Hogg goes to school but when he is on holiday he spends his time on the farm. Oh that boy! He is so wonderful. He does lots of tricks and cows like him too. You can tell it, for as soon as he appears they start staring at him. In no time they surround him each trying to sniff him. I think he actually talks to them.'

'Talk to cows! How can he do that when they do not even speak our language?' Helma asked with all curiosity.

'People think that animals are stupid but they are not. They are very intelligent. You see these ones here know their names. If I call out their names you will see them coming one by one.' He let one cow go and called out a name. The cow came. 'This one here is called Mama. Every one of them has a name.'

'Really? How do you know who is who? To me they all look the same.'

'They may look the same but they are different. Each one behaves differently too. You get to know how different they are when you spend time with them. I suppose they too, in their special way get to know who you are.'

Helma's concentration was broken by her aunt's call. She got up stretched her hand to Hardy saying, 'Thanks ever so much for telling me about cows. I will definitely come back here if not today tomorrow. You are a wonderful friend.'

Hardy too stood up and made a gentle bow to her. 'Much obliged Little Sis. See you soon.' He remained standing as

Helma disappeared around the corner. 'That is one good child in a million. I hope that is true.'

Mrs Hogg and Helma's parents were in the living room. In the kitchen Mr Hogg and his son were busy getting the meal ready. 'Come here gorgeous', Aunt Hogg called Helma. 'You have grown into a big girl. Come give your aunt a kiss.'

Helma kissed her on the cheek. She sat on the chair between her mother and aunt. 'Where is Heidi?' she asked.

'She and Nicky went down to the children's room. They must be playing or watching cartoons. You can join them if you want to but first I want you to greet your uncle and cousin.' She called out. 'Junior, Helma is here. Come along with you father too.'

Junior was a tall sturdy boy. He was ten but his physical build made him look like he was fifteen. Whenever his father was in charge of preparing dinner, Junior too spent time with him. He came in walking as gracefully as he always did. 'Here I am mother', he announced his arrival.

'Son, I want you to meet your cousin Helma.' She went on introduce them.

At the end of the introduction Junior bowed a little. 'Delighted to meet you, cousin Helma.'

Helma did not answer. She simply smiled as she held out her hand to shake his. The formalities were soon over, Junior returned to the kitchen. As for Helma, she sat by her mother waiting for her dinner.

# Helma the herds Girl

Helma had spent most of the night thinking about cows. Early the next morning, while everybody was still asleep, she ran down the farm to see the cows. Some were lying and others standing. Yet all of them seemed to be sleepy. She moved closer with the intention of touching one. As she drew closer she noticed that each one of them was actually chewing something in spite of the eyes being closed in sleep. She began to think aloud. 'This is strange. I have never before seen any creature sleep eating. May be I should say, this is the first time I see some creatures sleep eating. I wonder what they may be chewing.' She recalled the life in her home town, how people chewed gum on the trains and on buses. Then she burst in to her monologue again. 'Oh yes, I see it. I think human beings learnt how to chew sweets from cows. Or should I say, cows actually taught us to chew gum. Wait a minute! Are they really chewing gum?'

Junior approached rather noisily trying hard to avoid surprising Helma. 'Hello, Little Cousin; mind if I join you?' he asked.

'Of course not, if anything I am so glad you came because may be you can help me answer a few questions.'

'I will try but I must warn you I do not know all the answers' said Junior.

Helma did not wait. 'Where do you get all the sweets to give each cow? Surely, they must eat lots of them. Yesterday when they were being milked, I saw them chewing sweets. This morning I came here and what is more, they were sleeping but chewing gum. Tell me how much do they eat and who buys it?'

Junior did not laugh at Helma's lack of knowledge about cows. 'First of all, the cows are not chewing sweets. They chew the cud.'

'Does that mean every single day Uncle Hogg has to buy some curd? It must very expensive.'

Junior Hogg simply laughed. 'Cows are ruminants. That means they eat grass and bushes.'

'And chewing gum', interrupted Helma.

'Not chewing gum. They are simply chewing the curd', Junior started to explain. 'You see during the day and indeed any time when they come across good grass or food, they will eat as much as they can. They do not waste time chewing properly. Later on when they have had enough and are resting then they bring all the grass back and chew it properly so that it can be sent down to the next stomach. That is what they are doing now. They regurgitate the grass they did not chew properly. That is called chewing the cud.'

'What? Next stomach!'

'Oh yes, next stomach. All herb eating animals have four stomachs. When they eat they store their food in the first stomach where it waits until they chew it properly.'

Helma never broke her concentration. She watched the cows with increased interest. As for Junior, he was just another hero. He adored cows and seemed to talk to them. Even as he talked to Helma, he sat on one of them. 'Come and sit on this cow. She is friendly.' He put out his hand for the cow to lick. 'You see, she is very friendly.' Reluctantly Helma approached the cow. She put out her hand and felt the rough tongue of the cow on it.

'She is tickling me', she said.

'That is how her tongue feels. It is not like ours', explained Junior.

'Why is it rough?'

'I will show you in a minute', said Junior. He pushed his hand on the cow's jaw and gently lifted the skin off the mouth. 'Look here Little Sis! There are no teeth on upper jaw.'

Helma was rather surprised. 'How then do they cut the grass they eat?'

'They use their tongues. The tongue is wound around the grass and squeezed against the lower teeth.'

'But isn't it painful to chew grass without teeth.'

'I used to think that way too. But now I think it is alright. If it was painful they would not even try to eat it.'

'How did you get to know a lot about cows?' Helma asked.

'I guess it is from Hardy. He is a great lover of animals. He knows a lot and he has travelled to many countries in the world. He even told me lots of stories about African and Asian herdsmen.'

Helma had heard of Africa but had never given thought to what it was. What do African herdsmen do?'

This was something that he liked. Telling stories and his favourite was about the African herds boy called Bwana. He smiled and psyched himself into it. 'Some people depend on a cow for their livelihood. It provides food in the form of milk, blood and meat. Even the dung is never wasted. It is used as plaster for floors and walls. Some of it is dried and used as fuel for cooking and bonfires. In fact burning it they say repels mosquitoes. Some dung is used as manure.'

Junior's explanation held Helma's focus. Her silence urged him on. 'Among the native Africans known as Maasai, a cow is their most prized piece of wealth. Even when the cow dies, it continues to serve the people in form of clothing and sleeping mats. That is what they use the hide for.' He got up and walked with his cousin to the rocks on the far side of the farm. The sun was up and it was quiet nice to sit in. 'Long long ago', Junior begun. 'There lived a boy his name was Bwana. His parents were neither rich nor poor by their own standard. In fact they were considered wealthy because they had some ten heads of cattle. Bwana grew into such a family. He loved cattle so much such that he spent most of his time with them. He knew each cow and the cows knew him as well. He could tell what cow was ill and which one was happy. In fact people believed that the cows spoke to him.'

'Wait a minute', Helma broke in. 'But that is exactly what Hardy the herdsman told me about you. He said that all the cows know and like you too.'

'Well, I try to be like Bwana but I am nowhere closer. Any way shall I continue with the story?'

'Of course go on. I am sorry for having interrupted you', Helma apologised.

Junior continued. 'Bwana was really talented. Because he spent lots of time away from home he learnt to depend on cow milk for food. Milk was his breakfast, his lunch and his snack.'

'But how would he catch milk without a container?' Little Sis asked for fresh in her mind was the episode where Hardy was milking cows.

Junior paused to look at his cousin. Her eyes were fixed on him in attention. He knew she was expecting an answer. 'He did not need any container at all. Instead he relied on his friendship with cattle. He would simply cling between the cow's legs with his mouth sucking from the cow's udder. He was no different from a calf suckling.'

'Wow!' exclaimed Helma. 'He could really do that?'

'Yes', replied Junior. 'That Bwana would cling right under the cow with his mouth glued into the teats. He would only get off when he had had enough.' He paused and stole a quick glance at his cousin. There was no doubt that she was listening. Then he added. 'Personally, I think he was a great person who harvested only what he needed. Unlike our world where we take out too much but only to waste.'

The story had not only impressed Helma but also aroused her natural curiosity. More than ever she wanted to be like that herd's boy. She wanted to try it herself but she preferred to do it alone. Helma was still absorbing the story when Junior announced why he had come to the fields. 'Actually, I was sent to invite you for breakfast.'

'How did you know that I was here?'

'I just guessed.'

They walked back to the house together, Helma asking her questions and Junior answering them. But even then Helma's mind went back to the story of the little Maasai herds-boy. She was going to try his tricks and if possible become a herds-girl albeit only for the time she visited with the Hoggs. An opportunity came her way. Junior was gone for his private tuition. Her mother and aunt were in the house and even Hardy the herdsman had gone to his home for lunch. Helma did not waste time. 'I must try it. I must suckle the cow like

Bwana. When Junior comes back home, I will tell him all about it. Today, Junior will be proud of me', she told herself.

Well, she had no time to waste. She chose the very first cow she came across. She approached from the tails end and stood between the hind legs. At first the cow seemed to cooperate gently whacking her with its tail. Helma felt encouraged and actually tried to suckle the cow. Well, she tried her best but there was hardly any milk. 'Wrong cow, this one is. No milk in her', she muttered. 'May be some cows are not meant to give milk.'

She decided to try another cow. By this time the cow seemed to be even friendlier for even the tail was no longer stroking her. What Helma did not realise was that the cow was preparing to easy herself and in fact even the tail was already raised in position to leave open the exit ways. Whatever she was still doing came to a sudden stop when first all she felt like a bucket of lukewarm water was being thrown over her head. She jerked up to see what was going on. Unfortunately for her, everything had been badly timed. She was just recovering from the shock of cow urine when chunks of dung came down on her head. It spread through her face and on to her dress. She closed her eyes in submission letting the animal do its job. She was angry at herself. She was lost for words. She needed time to recover.

Helma hurried back determined to sneak into the house without being seen. She tried the back door first and found that it was locked. The windows too, they were locked or too high for her reach. The only option left was to go through the front door. Her clothes were soiled from cow dung and stinking too. 'I know what to do. I will just pretend that nothing happened. As for neighbours, that is their problem. I will simply ignore them', she told herself.

She quickly walked to the front door, careful not to draw attention from the neighbours. She reached for the door handle but it was locked. Everything seemed to work against her. Once again she had no choice but to ring the doorbell. She did just that and braced herself for the worst.

Mrs Hogg answered the doorbell. She glanced at Helma and fell into a litany of prayers. 'Blessed ancestors have mercy on us', she cried out. Then with hands akimbo she remarked, 'Little Woman that must be one hell of Halloween costume you got on you.' She stood there fighting laughter. 'I sincerely mean it although I must say that it is out of season. It stinks too making it perfect for scaring almost anyone.' She smiled sympathetically at Helma. 'What happened?'

'Some naughty cow chose to do its best on me. I mean it let go its mess on me.' There was a mixture of confident innocence and seriousness in her voice as she spoke. 'The animal has no manners. It could have just walked away to the toilet.'

'Well Little Woman, cows are not human beings. They have a tendency to drop their dung anywhere and without care.'

'But where Hardy was yesterday was very clean', protested Helma.

Mrs Hogg smiled. 'If you are talking about the milking sheds, well they too get messy. But Hardy takes care of it. He cleans it as soon as it happens.' She looked at her perplexed niece and concluded it was all down to blissful ignorance exasperated by Helma's ever presumptuous curiosity. 'Anyway step right in and if I were you I would run straight to the bathroom. You know what I mean.' She lowered her voice so that Helma's mother would not hear. 'We may as well tiptoe', she whispered.

Helma nodded in consent and started to head for the bathroom. Much to her disgust she met her mother in the corridor. 'Well, well. Girl, I think you have some explaining to do. What happened to your clothes?'

'Mother, it was not my fault. The cow did it. I just happened to be in the wrong place when its bowels opened. In short she let it go on me', stated Helma amid gasps of air.

'Now that is even more serious. Are you accusing the cow for doing what happens naturally?'

'Why did it have to do it on me? Surely it could have gone and done it somewhere else.'

The way she explained it and the tonality was sufficient to make anyone laugh. Mrs Pokrost knew she had to do what she always did best. She had to change the topic or find a way to water down the impact. 'Well, what is done is done. You just have to clean off that mess.'

'Okay mother', Helma said as she walked to the shower. Mrs Pokrost followed from behind with a mop to wipe off the mess that trailed Helma.

What on earth were you doing with cows?'

'Mother, I was sucking milk from its udder. I must have approached it from the wrong side let alone being a wrong cow', Helma begun with tears in her eyes. She went on to explain how she had dreamed of reliving the life of the legendary herds boy.

By now the rest of the children had joined in and were giggling away. 'Little Sis, you look beautiful in your costume. May I take your photograph', teased Heidi.

Mother had to abandon what she was doing to rescue Helma from the others. She was whisked to the bathroom. She took the dirty clothing to the outside house leaving Helma in the bathroom. By the time Mrs Pokrost returned Helma had already run a bath and was sitting in it. 'You can't do that because you will be wallowing in the same mess you are trying to get rid of.'

'But I like my bath', argued Helma.

'I know you do', answered Mrs Pokrost as she went ahead to unplug the stopper. 'The kind of mess you have on you required a shower. So get up and I will help you.'

As the shower run down her body, Helma realised why her mother had insisted on it. A stream of grime was hurrying to the drain. Several minutes later Helma emerged in clean clothing. Even then, the other children did not forget the event. They started to call her, Miss Little Herds-girl. She did not mind the title. If anything she was glad she had earned it and had learnt a little bit more about cows.

Later that evening as the family sat reminiscing events of the day, Helma happily shared her experience of the day. 'I am grateful to the cow that did its business on me; she began.

By now everyone was laughing. She waited for the laughter to die out and continued. 'The truth is that, thanks to the experience I have actually come with a business idea. Uncle Hogg, this proposition is going to mint us all the money we need.'

Helma had everybody's attention. 'What is the business proposition?' asked Uncle Hogg.

'I think we should invest on diapers for farm animals. Not only will it keep the place clean but it will also mean that any dung is safely emptied in some specially prepared spots. More details later.' With that she ended her business proposition and quietly sat while the rest rolled with laughter.

Milton Keynes UK
Ingram Content Group UK Ltd.
UKHW050128180724
445705UK00010B/111

9 781803 695792